T0113606

MID-NIGHT MURDER

TENDER RONI

authorHOUSE®

AuthorHouse™
1663 Liberty Drive
Bloomington, IN 47403
www.authorhouse.com
Phone: 833-262-8899

Published by AuthorHouse 04/20/2021

ISBN: 978-1-7283-6811-5 (sc)
ISBN: 978-1-7283-6810-8 (e)

Print information available on the last page.

This is a work of fiction. All of the characters, names, incidents, organizations, and dialogue in this novel are either the products of the author's imagination or are used fictitiously.

This book is printed on acid-free paper.

"An chilling and emotionally charged story that readers can find to be compelling and disturbing."

"A novel about what it means to be a African American boy or man at our time, but not exclusively for just African American boys or men. This can be for any reader once you pick this book up, it becomes a part of you where you ponder about what really happen."

MID-NIGHT MURDER

Georgia, known to be as the peach state of the world. Often called the Empire State of the south. Georgia is also known for many things such as music films, soul foods, and beautiful historic landmarks. Georgia consist of 159 counties with Dekalb being the birth place for Stone Mountain Park.

Living in a city like Dekalb it has it rewards and its disadvantages. When one decide to move to Dekalb County one has to be aware of the crime rate, and there economic class and where exactly to fit into a county full of different races.There is a place we all can easily fit in this big county. One can decide to be among the working class or part of the criminal system. We as members of this beautiful community fight to keep our county safe for children and families to grow. Unfortunately, you going have things that just don't belong. It takes good citizens of this world to take out the pieces that don't belong and replace them with good ones to make our county, our city, our streets safe and more inviting.

Being a neighborhood drug dealer doesn't award our community the safest place to live. We desire to be a county where our children can play safely and feel good about where they live. If one chooses to sell drugs or illegal substances have made the choice to take on the consequences that come with the crime.

CONTENTS

CHAPTER 1

CHILDHOOD STRUGGLES

Boom! Boom! Boom! The sound of the bullets leaving the chamber of Edward F. Maxwell's loaded pistol echoed through the surrounding neighborhoods as they traveled towards three frightened teenagers. Unfortunately, they were in the wrong place at the worse time. First, let's look at Edward Maxwell's history in order to understand why he would attack three defenseless teens.

Given the name "Head" at a young age, he was known as the boy with a round head and a very slender built body. Edward's head was always known to be very disproportionate to his body. Although his head was pretty big, his size paled in comparison to the other kids his age. Nevertheless, the name "Head" stuck with him, and so did his troubles. Like many kids around the world, Edward came face-to-face with his parent's inner demons.

At the age of 8, he was acclimated to the absence of his father from his life. His mother Rachel, with little education, dropped out of high school to care for her son with the help of welfare and other public assistance. She was Edward's only role model. Being a single mother, she was constantly in and out of relationships with different men. Although Edward didn't recognize it, he was desperate for a male role model so he would emulate the men in his mother's life; a behavior that would later cause problems. Sadly, these men, driven by rage and jealousy, were prone to extreme violence when dealing with Rachel. Sometimes all it took was for her to disobey a simple order to bring about violence; violence that would get so bad, that a man shut both of his mother's eyes. Edward recalled seeing another boyfriend set his mother's car on fire. This was done out of sheer vengeance. He hated seeing his mother put herself in these situations. Rachel was a beautiful loving and very petite lady, who always wore her hair short. She was very assertive and bossy, at least that's how Edward remembered her. She was the type of woman that wanted and seized control over any and every situation. She sometimes got into arguments or even fistfights because of her quick-temper. That's why it broke him up inside all the more to see his mother controlled and violently abused by numerous men. Those were memories he could never forget.

Due to the domestic abuse, Rachel and her partners constantly had run-ins with the law. By the time Edward was 8 years old, he was already accustomed to his mom being in the backseat of police cars and the inside of jail cells. His mother was once again arrested on drug trafficking charges and sentenced to 5 years in prison, which left Edward in the care of his grandmother. With no real role model at home and a lackadaisical grandmother, Edward looked to the streets of Miami for the guidance he was not getting at home. At such a young age, he couldn't make sense of the events that had taken his mother away from him, or the loneliness he felt at being abandoned by his father and deserted by his mother. This set the stage for Edward's own run-ins with the law.

While living with his grandmother, Edward was visited occasionally by his father. Edward's father was known in the community as a "street hustler" who dubbed the moniker "Mid Night" because of his dark skin and the criminal activities he committed in the dead of night. Those crimes ranged from robberies, shootings, and home invasions. Having the tendency to quickly transition from a fistfight to a shootout, Edward's father was also known as "Billie the Badass". Around the time Edward turned 10 and into his late pre-teens, he would ride out with his father through the streets of Over-Town. He saw his father sell drugs, shoot craps and chase away drug addicts. Edward could vividly recall a very chilling incident when his dad took him to a "crap house". He witnessed his dad fire a gun at a man he believed was attempting to rob him. However, Edward wasn't really sure if the bullet actually hit the man. He remembered the car ride back to his grandmother's house and that his father didn't actually have a place to stay. Hanging out with his dad was not a pleasant experience, but living with his grandmother wasn't much better. Edward would watch his grandmother receive verbal abuse from his grandfather, who was also cheating on her, which led to constant fights. But if that didn't make him feel uncomfortable enough, Edward was also subjected to abuse from his older cousins who punched and kicked him around. They also teased him about his mom and dad being absent in his life and saying it was because they didn't want him. Edward despised living at his grandmother's house and dreamed to once again live with his mother. He found himself writing to his mother in prison occasionally, urging her to come and get him and take him home. However, after writing several letters and getting no response, he eventually gave up hope that his words were reaching his mother. He felt unloved and forgotten by his mother. Edward later found out that his grandmother was hiding his mother's letters to him and telling him that she hasn't written back.

He had never forgotten his aunt, his mother's sister, Shaneice, and how he wanted to live with her so badly. She was a single mother in college with one daughter, trying hard to make a better life for her. Sometimes she would come and get him and he would get the chance to experience her very "conventional" style of living. His Aunt Shaneice lived a very normal life and only had good things to say about his mother Rachel. On their long car rides or their trips to the shopping mall, Shaneice would tell Edward about how his mother made a bad decision. She would reassure him that after his mother was done serving her time, she would be back to get him. His aunt disliked dropping him back off at his grandmother's house and wanted to do more to help him, but she lacked experience in dealing with troubled children. Besides, Shaneice had enough on her hands raising her own child while in school. His aunt eventually moved further away to Austell, Georgia to provide a better life for her 10-year-old child. She had moved into a nice three-bedroom house, with enough space for her sister to move in once she was released from prison; an offer her sister accepted, leaving her home in Florida and traveling north. Edward eventually followed his mother to Georgia as well.

Edward moved to Georgia to escape the horrible circumstances he faced in Florida, hoping to find a better life with his mother and aunt in a new place. Little did he know that he could not escape from his past and problems because they had already manifested themselves within him. Things were going well for him over the first couple of months, but Edward began to find himself at odds with just about everyone, starting with the students at his school. He faced expulsion multiple times due to his violent demeanor and tendency to get into physical altercations. Edward was expelled from the local elementary school and, eventually, every school in Dekalb County. That behavior wasn't only limited to school; he would often cause disruptions at home, being combative with his mother and aunt in an attempt to gain control of the house. He had developed the mindset that he was the man of the house, despite his aunt's reluctance to that attitude and the strong stand she took against him. The power struggles started to become egregious, to the point of physical violence. There was even an instance where his aunt and mother broke a broom off of his back, in an attempt to gain control, to no success.

Moving Back to Florida

Feeling remorse at the prospect of not being able to control her son's behavior, Edward's mother decided to move her son and herself back to Florida so Edward couldn't cause any more problems for her sister and niece. She moved in with her mother Mrs. Mae, a sort of "safe haven" for the family, where they would travel to when times got rough. By Edward's 18th birthday, he had no diploma, no job and no driver's license. The only thing he owned was a bag of clothes that he shuffled around with him while he conducted his "business" in the dangerous streets of Florida. He loitered on street corners, occasionally gambling and frequenting strip clubs. There were times when his gambling would become almost lethal, such as the time he was shot in his left shoulder after attempting to skip out on a bet. His mother couldn't steer him from trouble because she was still struggling to get her life together as she found herself with two more children that needed all of her attention. She couldn't help him herself, but that didn't stop her from trying to get help for him. She tried many options, even taking him to church, hoping the prayers would change something in him, but it might have already been too late. The streets had claimed him.

Edward's parents were unsure what to do with him, for he had no particular skills, no education, no experience, and no job or even a willingness to work. The only option they could come up with that would be beneficial to both Edward and his parents, was for him to feign mental instability in an attempt to qualify for a mental disability check from the government. His parents had instructed him to act insane in front of the "reviewers" from the state, even going as far as to prepare a script detailing the things he should say and do while the "reviewer" was present. Feeling unable to care for himself, Edward reluctantly agreed to the ploy. He would go into his doctor's appointment with claims of hearing voices, extreme paranoia, and incessant restlessness. His doctor prescribed medicine for conditions Edward completely fabricated, but it earned him the $736 disability check that he sought after and the attention and care his mother wanted for him.

Unable to receive the money herself, Rachel confided in her mother to be the recipient of the check. Edward felt it was an easy way to access the money the state awarded him and would call his grandmother up on the first of every month and persuade her to withdraw the money and give it to him in cash. Unaccustomed to having a large sum of cash on him, Edward made bad decisions with his money. The money would be split between marijuana, strip clubs, and the streets of Florida. Occasionally, he would take his money and buy the newest pair of Jordan's shoes or clothes. Unable to wait to put them on, he would put on the clothing and leave his current clothing in the store. Sometimes refusing to go to a dressing room, he would put on the clothes where he stood in front of the other customers. Edward couldn't tell if he had started to feel the effects of the medication he was taking or if he was just seeking attention.

CHAPTER 2

MOVE BACK TO GEORGIA

Rachel decided to give living in Georgia another try. Only this time, she would leave her troublesome son behind to the drug and gang infested streets of Florida. So, she and her two little children went off looking for a better and safer life in Georgia. Besides, Rachel felt that Edward was an adult now and capable of taking care of himself with the support of his disability check.

Edward's disability check wasn't enough for him to live on his own so he found himself living with his grandparents, sleeping on their floor, couch, or even up against a wall at times, wherever he could find space at his grandparents' place. Most of the time, he would take chances staying at his Aunt Keisha's apartment in Winter Gardens, despite the fact that he was not on the lease. His aunt lived in a two-bedroom apartment passed down from her mother, and having Edward living there violated her public housing lease agreement, so Edward was never allowed to stay longer than two or three weeks at most for fear of being reported.

But despite residing there only briefly, and the fact that he was told to keep a low profile, he had made himself quite visible. Whether it was physical altercations with the local gangs or just hanging around the gambling hole with shady individuals, Edward had begun to build a negative reputation for himself and, indirectly, for his aunt as well. His aunt Keisha was the youngest of his mother's sisters and she lived a very quiet and reclusive lifestyle. She was known to be humble in spirit, meek, and gentle, which is a stark contrast to Edward. His actions only annoyed and angered her because he was upending her way of life.

Edward seemed to possess the skills to find trouble, wherever it rested, though he never had to travel far to find it. Trouble would usually come in the form of gambling in "crap" games. Edward was confident in the skills he nurtured while rolling dice with his dad. His dad's advice was always "Whether you win or lose, get your money and go". Following his dad's advice, Edward found himself engaging in one particular midnight "crap" game where the only individuals out gambling that night were those that were either looking for trouble, already in trouble, or just getting out of trouble.

Edward tried his luck at rolling the dice, but unfortunately, his luck failed him that night and it was time to empty his pockets, according to the spoken agreement they all had made. Emptying his pockets was something that went against his dad's training, so, when it came time to pay up, Edward ran. Immediately there were gunshots, all of which missed him, except for one bullet. That bullet struck him in his right shoulder causing his body to fall to the ground, going limp. The men all fled leaving Edward lying there bleeding and writhing in pain. An ambulance showed up shortly afterward, transporting Edward to the nearest Florida Hospital.

The doctors were able to stabilize him but felt it would be best that they leave the bullet in his shoulder due to health concerns. It was at that point, laying in the hospital bed, that Edward began to reevaluate his life. He did something that he had not done in a long time, He begin to pray. Edward called out to God and then to his mother. His mother rushed to his side and within a couple of days he was released from the hospital.

Even after that incident, Edward still could not keep himself out of trouble. It had even gotten to the point where his dad, the source of a lot of his bad habits, couldn't stand the sight of his own son. Edward was known to start fights with his mother, grandmother, and aunts and they all blamed his dad. Edward was becoming too much like his dad and he couldn't tolerate it.

Daddy Against Son

Now an adult, Edward couldn't care less about gaining or giving respect to his dad anymore. He was no longer afraid of the consequences of standing up to his parents, especially his dad, as he was sure to mention it to him over the phone. Whenever they talked, the conversation was never pleasant and often ended in threats of extreme violence. Edward and his dad somehow managed to avoid each other, despite frequenting the same spots. Things went on like that for a while until his dad showed up at his Aunt Keisha's house after learning that Edward spends most of his time there. He knocked on the door and proceeded to yell Edward's name, urging him to come outside. His dad's intentions were purely violent and was apparent by the tone of his voice and the obscenities he was yelling.

Edward would have bolted out the door immediately but his aunt was holding him back. She didn't want the attention that a physical altercation on her doorsteps would draw. His dad started to become agitated because Edward wouldn't come outside. Seeing Edward stare at him from the window, made him even more irate. Edward's dad ran up to the window and punched out the glass, saying "Don't make me come in there and get you". At this point, Edward had enough and ran right out the front door to confront his dad.

All the neighbors and local gangs had proceeded to leave their apartments and gather around to see what all the commotion was about. The fight between dad and son had started and blow after blow was being exchanged between the two men. It was very clear that Edward was losing the battle as his face and shirt became soaked in blood. Edward's dad had pinned him to the ground and was choking the life from him. Seeing Edward losing his battle had galvanized the local gang members to support him in his fight. A group of nine or ten men pulled Edward's dad off of him and proceeded to attack him. In the midst of the chaos, Edward escaped to his aunt's apartment. His dad was now pinned on the ground receiving blow after blow from the men, targeting his head, ribs, and every other inch of his body that they could hit. The assault on Edward's dad continued until the men heard sirens in the distance and tires coming to a screeching halt of the scene. His dad left the scene on a stretcher heading to the hospital. Edward was also taken to the hospital as a result of the fight with his dad. Both dad and son were released from the hospital around the same time and seemingly went their separate ways. However, a few days later Edward started to receive phone calls from his dad, calls relaying messages that their little feud wasn't over and that he was going to kill him.

With a death threat looming over Edward's head, no one wanted Edward to be around, for they feared for their safety and the safety of their families. Edward's aunt was thoroughly discontent with the events he had put her through and finally put her foot down and told Edward that he could no longer spend nights at her place because it would put her and her daughter in danger. She also feared being kicked out of her apartment. Every family member Edward encounter held similar stances and he soon found himself with nowhere to go. They tried to convince him that leaving the state would be the best thing for him to do. But he had no transportation, no plan, and at that very moment, nowhere to spend the night.

Edward remembered that the hospital had him on file as a patient with a very serious schizophrenia bipolar disorder so he started checking himself in as a patient. The hospital would house him for a few nights at a time, feeding him and providing him with a nice hot shower. The hospital was the only place he could sleep peacefully so he would frequently check himself in and the staff at the hospital became very familiar with him. Edward continued this process until he received his disability check. So with his duffle in hand he headed to the nearest Greyhound Bus Station and boarded the first bus to Atlanta and he never looked back!

CHAPTER 3

THE NEIGHBORHOOD DRUG DEALER

Rachel was back in Georgia with one of her children, her baby boy Charles, to hopefully find a new beginning. Edward saw an opportunity and seized it, moving in with Rachel and Charles. But instead of searching for a new beginning for himself, he slumped into the same old shady things that he was already familiar with. Edward's job, hobby, and pastime became dealing drugs. He refused to search for a legitimate job or even take classes to obtain a GED.

Unfortunately, Edward was able to find sufficient clientele for his illegal dealings. In that predominantly black neighborhood of Georgia, most of the inhabitants were chronic weed smokers, providing Edward a market in which his product was in high demand. He always carried his "stash" of drugs on him, for convenience's sake, when he sold marijuana to the younger teens and their parents in the neighborhood, along with pills and moonshine. Drug trafficking became a daily routine with the same clientele. Anyone moving outside of the routine was deemed, suspects.

Rachel house was situated right on the corner of a four-way intersection, in plain sight of everyone. The bright yellow house with white trimmings met with a long driveway extending from in front of its two-car garage. A small porch fixated on the front of the house would lead to a lawn with freshly cut grass. The house was plainly visible, not only to those looking for drugs, but to everyone. In the neighborhood, the bright yellow house with its white trim became known as the "weed man's house".

Rachel found work at the local waffle house and contributed to the household income. Charles didn't have a need to work because he received a social security check monthly. He was compensated regularly for the lethal actions of a drunk driver that claimed the life of his father when he was very young.

Edward still received his disability check, which he used to restock his drug supply. As time went on, Edward began to increase his selection of drugs, which included popular drugs like "Ganja", "Mary Jane", "Chronic", "Cush", "Mollies", and Percocet, just to name a few. For all of Edward's shortcomings, bad quality drugs couldn't be considered one of them. He was known to have the best quality when it came to marijuana or other drugs; a status that he was proud of and maintained. This was his lifestyle. This was how he survived and how he helped to put food on the table.

Edward was a professional drug dealer and had rules for his business. He would never meet anyone at the front door and did not allow them to step foot in his yard. The meet-up spot was always either at the corner or around the block. No one would ever make the mistake of meeting him at his front door, or in his yard. They would watch from the street, or park on the side of the road, but never in the driveway.

The Break-In

Word got out, months before the party, that Edward's house had been broken into. It was said that his back door was kicked open by a couple of teens on a dark cold night in October. The disabled neighbor living to the left of them had spotted a group of three teens in the driveway. He noted that they arrived around 6:00 pm and exited a four-door Toyota Camry with a dark tint on their windows. They were all wearing hoodies, but all had noticeable distinctions. One was tall and slender with an afro, which he chose to conceal with a hoodie after stepping out onto the driveway.

The other two wore their hoodies over their heads on the ride there. The taller teen wore a black hoodie with the letters MECA on the front of it. He also sported black jeans and black Nike Air Force Ones. The second oldest of the three teens wore a plain red hoodie with stonewashed jeans and a blue handkerchief hanging from his back pocket and wore brown Timberland boots. The last one straggled behind the other two wearing a hoodie with a picture of Tupac on it, khakis and black high-top sneakers. He had chosen not to wear a belt and therefore struggled to keep his pants up as he ran to the back door where the other two waited.

The neighbor, peering out of the crack between his curtains in his upstairs bedroom, watched as they slipped into the darkness behind the house. He assumed that they might be family coming to visit, or new residents of the house. Even still, he knew that he had never seen them before and decided that he'd watch on. It never dawned on him that at that moment a break-in was in progress, that was not until he heard the sounds of a wooden door cracking under the pressure of a heavy boot pounding against it.

"BOOM" went the initial strike, followed by two and then three other rapid outbursts until the frame gave way and the door flew open, losing a glass pane that shattered on the floor in the entrance of the doorway. They ran past the kitchen and living area, knowing full well that the valuables were stored upstairs. The three teens spotted a 49" flat screen mounted onto the wall in the master bedroom and attempted to remove it with little success, wasting costly minutes. Finally, giving up on the TV, they moved to the dressers in every room, tossing anything that didn't look valuable out. Suddenly, they came across a similar smaller TV, headphones, a Wii console, games, a boom box, a radio and other valuables that they were able to carry off in their hands. One of the rooms was empty with the exception of a few boxes and bags of clothes, feeling it would be a waste of time, they did not search that room.

With the stolen items in hand, they fled out the front door leaving it slightly open and unlocked before jumping into their car and roaring off down the street. The burglary took all of thirty minutes.

Rachel, Edward's mom, was the first to return home, as she always did, at 7:00PM. Approaching her house, she could immediately tell that something was amiss. She noticed that the front door was left slightly open, a mistake that neither she or her sons would make. Rachel went to the neighbors' house looking for someone to do a walkthrough with her, as she believed that there might be someone in her home. Appearing to be a bodybuilder, the neighbor that lived to the right of her was a massive guy. He walked Rachel back to her place, leading the way through the opened front door. Making it halfway past the living room he looked back to meet Rachel's gaze. She looked past him to see her back door hanging off the hinges and it had become undeniably clear, she had been robbed! Cautioning her to stay behind him, he led the way up the stairs. Entering the master bedroom first, they noticed that the robbers had left the room in shambles, taking special notice to the fact that the flat screen remained in the room after stubbornly resisting to be removed from the wall. Rachel then went from room to room, making a list of all the things that were missing. Crestfallen, she slowly made her way downstairs to meet the police that were arriving.

Four squad cars arrived at Rachel's residence to canvas the scene and look for evidence. They dusted for fingerprints and took pictures of anything they felt might be useful in the case. The flat-screen TV that was left behind was covered in finger prints, which were uncovered by the police officers. After the sweep of the house, the private detective took statements from witnesses that claimed to have seen what actually happened. With the evidence and witness statements, they were able to identify one of the teens.

Rachel received a letter in the mail suggesting that she appear in court to press charges against the teen, but she was reluctant to do so. She felt that it would be pointless unless all of the perpetrators were caught. Rachel also worried that if she spoke out against him before all of the burglars were caught and convicted, she would be in danger of retaliation. She didn't believe they would grant her witness protection, so it wasn't worth her time to appear in court. Reports about other break-ins around the neighborhood had quickly circulated and they believed that it was the same group of teens. Rachel figured that if they kept up the burglaries, it wouldn't be long before she would get justice.

CHAPTER 4

THE PARTY

There was a huge party in the works somewhere on Chapel Hill Road, which was set to take place on June 13, 2014 and everyone knew about it. The online registration made it easy to see who was going to attend, and the numbers just kept rising. It was a backyard 'Bring Your Own Bottle' (BYOB) party with lots of food, liquor, and hookahs, all on a quarter acre of land. Multiple tables for dominos, beer pong, food, and hookah smokers had already been set up. Twan and his sister Keona were hosting the party and took part in setting everything up. A massive crowd was expected and arrangements had been made to accommodate the large crowd; even opening up and clearing out the garage in case the party spilled out into other areas. The house door was left open for party-goers to access the food that was in the kitchen, which consisted of an assortment of meats, salads, rice, and cakes.

Taking the back door out of the kitchen led you right next to DJ Twan where he had his iPod connected to his sound system, blasting out the latest tunes to keep people on their feet and dancing. Tiffany was bartending just a table away, making sure that everyone stayed in high spirits. She was very skilled at mixing drinks as was evident by the drove of people patiently waiting in line to receive a drink. Her supply of liquor came from the bottles that everyone brought with them, so her alcohol stock was entirely exotic and colorful, which kept plenty of partygoers at the bartender's table.

The party was a going-away party for Keona. She and Twan had already moved into a new house across town but they wanted to have a little unsupervised fun before leaving the house that they had lived in for the past decade. At the time of the party, everything had been removed from the house except a refrigerator, a couple of chairs, and a pool table. Even the lights and water were still on when the party occurred, which was a big plus. The party had been planned by Keona as a goodbye to the neighbors she had grown up with, as well as the girls whose hair she had styled throughout the years. Her brother helped set up the party while her aunt provided the food. The color scheme was black and orange, which mimicked the balloons on the mailbox out front, the tents outback, and the cake in the kitchen. Keona was excited to be throwing this party and didn't care who showed up, as long as they showed up in masses. She wanted around three hundred people to attend, so she commissioned her brother to reach out via Facebook blast, Instagram posts, and twitter blast. And it worked because Keona noticed cars lining up along the curb of their house.

People were filing in by the dozens as bottles started to line the bartender's table. Music blasted from the speakers and attracted all the locals to the backyard. Everyone was dancing or drinking, or doing a little bit of both and it wasn't long before a soul train line was formed. While the party was going on in the back, Aunt Sand kept an eye on the front of the house and made sure that everyone who arrived found their way to the back. She was really a cool, down to earth person and was indistinguishable from the other young party-goers and blended right in at the party. Aunt Sand was cool, but very responsible. Before the party even began, she had discussed some ground rules to be adhered to with Keona. One of them being that people could not be out front, especially if they were smoking or drinking. Parking directions and instructions for her party guests were also in place to ensure that the party would not be in jeopardy of being shut down.

The setting and mode of the party were perfect for Keona. In one corner was the bar where people were getting drunk and a little bit rowdy. Adjacent to the bar were tables for playing cards. The card players were also causing quite a commotion, especially the spade players where a notorious champion emerged amongst them, going by the name of Jace. One area of the party was shrouded in smoke as you approached the smoking tables where the hookahs were located. The hookah smokers were having a pretty casual and quiet conversation.

Keona was elated at how the party turned out as talk, laughter, and chants echoed throughout the packed party. If there was one thing that she didn't like about the party, it would have to be one very unwelcome guest named Tammie. Tammie was known by the title "Old Lady Hoe" due to the fact that she flirted with the young men at the party, despite being in her late forties, pushing close fifty. She had worked hard on her body after living her younger years as a heavy set woman and she loved to show it off. Tammie did everything she could to get the young men's attention, which included wearing a short (short) dress. She had a pretty large selection to choose from because most of the men there were single. Other than Tammy, Keona was weary of the "Florida Squad" who spoke only about Miami and Pensacola. They hung out with each other and only engaged in intermingling, cutting themselves off from the rest of the party.

The Curfew

Around 11:30, Orlando, Orandeys' brother, arrived at the party and was followed shortly thereafter by their mutual friend Boo. Andre came to Orandey looking for marijuana after having been smoking all day. Orandey was reluctant at first but got into Orlando's car with Andre while Orlando headed toward the doorway to get Larry home because Orlando was noticeably drunk. Orlando asked if Orandey could take the wheel and drop Larry off home. After spending all day with Larry, Orlando was instructed to have him home by a certain time. Larry was the youngest of their crew, being just 15yrs old at the time, he came to know Orlando after playing basketball with him at the neighborhood courts. Not having an older male in his family to look up to, Larry really admired Orlando and wanted to followed in his footsteps. Larry had a very strict mother and in order to hang out with Orlando, he needed her approval. Although his mother lived "in the hood", she wouldn't let her residence define her, her family, or her household. She was a teacher at Mountain Creek High School where her son attended. Mountain Creek High, although it was a public school, it operated similar to a private school with accelerated and advanced placement courses, a distinct uniform, and a rigorous curriculum. Most of the values and morals they implemented at the school, she instilled those same values and morals into her own kids as well. Orlando knew it would be a tall task to convince Larry's mother to let him attend Keona's party, so they went with a convincing lie. They told her that there would be no drugs or alcohol and plenty of adult supervision, which, of course, was the furthest thing from the truth. But Orlando ensured her that he would look after Larry. Larry's mother looked Orlando square in the face, making sure she had complete eye contact and his undivided attention and said to him, "I'm trusting you with my boy. He can go to this party this one time, but he has a curfew and must be home by 1:00am at the latest", she warned. "Not 1:30AM, or 2:00AM, but 1:00AM! You can bring him back earlier if you want, but no later than 1:00. You are fully responsible for him, and he is not to leave or ride off with anyone else. You are responsible for getting him home safely", she added. "Do we have an understanding?" She took one more long look into Orlando's eyes for confirmation before allowing Larry to leave with him.

CHAPTER 5

THE DRIVE TO EDWARD'S HOUSE

Tuesday night was pretty warm and sticky with a temperature of 83 degrees and a humidity of 70. The sky was dark with the exception of a few clusters of clouds that were dimly lit by the almost lavender hue of the full moon. The three had left Keona's party to buy some weed for Andre from Edward. Edward's house was in walking distance from the party, but Andre decided to ditch his bike to get a ride from Orandey. Orlando, too drunk to drive, passed the keys to Orandey. They were driving their mother's black Hyundai. They paused for a few moments in the driveway before they departed, making Larry a little nervous. The clock was ticking and they were nowhere near his residence. He kept thinking, "maybe I should text my mom, but what would I tell her?". He thought maybe he should tell her that he's on the way, or that he was leaving now. It wasn't until Orandey turned the radio on to 97.9, that Larry started to relax. They were playing "Try Me" by Def Loaf and everyone was enjoying the music. Larry almost didn't notice that it was already 1 o'clock. By this time, Andre had hopped into the back seat of the car and there was this vibe to the music. Andre was carrying a loaded pistol on him, and, because of the way he was sitting, he relocated it from one pocket to the next, an action neither Orandey nor Larry noticed. Andre began to notice they hadn't moved yet and yelled, "Damn man what are we waiting for?". And with that, Orandey began to back out of the driveway.

Orandey wanted to get Larry home and hurry back to the party so that he wouldn't miss anything. "Let's make this snappy so I can get back," he urged Andre. They pulled up to Ed's house, which was on the way. Pulling into the neighborhood, they took note of certain things like the neighbors returning home and the cars in Edward's driveway. They saw a Ford pick-up truck, a 1976 Chevy Cutlass, and a man getting out of his blue Grand Am. Waiting out front while the stranger went inside, the setting was a little too ominous for Andre that night.

Orandey and Larry started up a little small talk to change the mood. Orandey had asked Larry about the girls at the party and whether or not he got any of their phone numbers. Larry immediately brought up a girl named Lisa, which prompted Andre to join the conversation, insisting that he had already been with Lisa a few months back, claiming that she was a psycho. Talk started to die down as the man left the house. "Back into the driveway, and turn off your lights and music," Andre instructed. After Orandey backed into the driveway, Andre asked for his phone as he set there with his head hung low. Orandey turned off the lights, but kept the music playing at a medium volume. All the while, Larry still worried about his curfew, realizing that they were well past it. At this point, he didn't know how much longer it was going to take and was too scared to call his mother.

Andre wanted to let Edward know that they were outside, but couldn't find his contact in Orandey's phone. Handing the phone back to Orandey, asked him for Edward's number. Orandey passed the phone back after finding the contact in his phone as the "Weed Man". At this point, Andre had removed the Smith and Wesson black and silver .40 caliber pistol from his pocket and had it laying on his lap, a move Orandey nor Larry noticed, as they stayed facing forward.

It was 1:30 in the morning when Edward got Andre's call. He was sprawled out on the couch and everyone else was sleeping in their beds. It was the usual late-night call that he's come to expect from his frequent customers. It was never unusual to receive calls from an unknown number at any time of the day. Within a split second of him answering the call, he was greeted with a loud "Yo I'm outside". The voice sounded familiar, so he peeked out of his blinds to see a black car backed into the driveway. The car was unfamiliar to him and the fact that the lights were off but the car was still running raised a few alarms in Edward's head. He ran upstairs to his bedroom to retrieve his revolver from his top drawer. The revolver had a deep black handle and a chamber that held .5 caliber rounds. Edward then went back downstairs, peeking out of the blinds, making certain they were still there. With his phone in one hand and gun in the other, he stepped outside to examine the three dark figures in the car.

Edward was wearing a button-down shirt left unbuttoned with a white T-shirt underneath and black jeans paired with black Air Force One's. As he stood on his porch, he went through many scenarios on what he should do. Does he shoot first and ask questions later? Does he wake up his family and alert them to the people in the driveway? Or, does he call the cops and let them deal with it? The last option seemed off the table because he knew the cops would question why they were there and at the moment, Edward knew, he had too much marijuana in the house. He had considered walking back inside and giving his mother one last kiss before approaching the car. Then the thug in him popped out as he decided he'd handle it on his own and walked towards the car with his revolver aimed. He made a wide arc to try and see the faces of the driver and his passengers. He made out the faces of Andre and a younger guy and moving closer, he was able to see Andre face and even the outfit he had worn when he visited earlier.

Edward walked directly behind the car to the back passenger seat, finger still on the trigger. "Andre, what's up?" he uttered. Andre looked up at him and yelled, "Man, my weed is short!".

CHAPTER 6

SHOTS FIRED!

Orandey was stiff, sitting upright and facing forward with his foot above the gas. He was ready to take off on a moment's notice if need be. Glancing up in the rearview mirror, Orandey noticed Edward heading around to the window where Andre was seated. The engine had almost completely muffled their conversation, that was until Edward started to raise his voice. Andre made claims that Edward had shorted him on his supply:

"Man the weed you gave me was short" claimed Andre.

"Where's the blunt Andre?"

"I don't have it", Andre responded quickly.

"Well you better get the fuck outta here", yelled Edward.

By this point both Andre and Edward were upset. Andre grabbed and lifted his pistol up until it was level with Edward's head. Without thinking, Edward let loose all of his rounds. The first round struck Andre in the nose, while the second was buried into his chest. Edward didn't stop there for he wanted to make sure that there wouldn't be any chance of retaliation. His bullets traveled towards Orandey, striking him in the face and the neck. Orandey foot had eased off of the brakes as he lost feeling in his body. The car slowly crept forward while Edward continued shooting, moving his aim to Larry. Larry ducked, cradling himself in the seat to protect his body. He was shot multiple times on his left side, once in his abdomen another in his thigh and chest. Edward repeatedly fired his revolver until he was out of bullets, backing away as he did it.

Miraculously, Andre escaped the car and headed through the neighbors' front yards, slowly weaving through vehicles as he yelled for help. He had crawled his way up to the neighbor's vehicle leaning on it trying to make his way to the steps, no strength to run or even stand; he attempted to twist the doorknob, in a vain attempting to escape to the safety of the house. His struggles left bloodstains all over the neighbor's door and with no fight left in him, he laid there, motionless. Blood had begun to pool around him, and he could only siphon enough strength to just barely mutter the phrase, "Help Me". The neighbor, sitting on the other side of the door, told him that he had called the police and that help was on the way. The neighbor took a looking at his clock, the neighbor saw that the time was five minutes before 2 am.

Andre was in pretty bad shape, listing powerlessly from side to side, unable to keep his body up but was able to find and pull the door handle, spilling out onto the concrete. He could slightly hear crying and groans coming from the passenger seat where Larry sat. Orandey called out to Larry trying to confirm that he was there and okay. "Yeah man I'm here, I can't find my phone to call the police, and I've been shot," Larry shouted back. Orandey didn't have his phone either and didn't have the strength to look for help. Larry slipped out of the vehicle, which was now in the middle of the street, and headed up towards the top of the street and was able to stop a lady who was on her way home, his apparent state shocking her greatly, he convinced her to call for help. She could see a person collapsed on a porch, and another person collapsed in the middle of the street next to a stalled vehicle. She could hear a faint call for help.

"Don't move, help is on the way!"

Edward snuck his way around the crime scene that he had created, finding Andre in front of his neighbor's door. Pulling the cell phone from his pocket, he called a friend to pick him up. Edward explained how he had to shoot a couple of guys to protect himself, and now he had to escape the scene. Before his ride arrived, Edward moved over to Larry who was now lying on the ground and wiped the handle and barrel of the gun with his shirt and held it to Larry's hands, moving his fingers all along the revolver multiple times. He then discarded the gun in the grass of his front yard, a few yards away from the boys. Edward paced back and forth, fumbling with the idea of leaving. Taking his phone out of his pocket, he dialed 911, stating that there had been a shooting on his block. He began to feign ignorance to the whole situation, claiming only to be a bystander to the events that had occurred right outside his door.

When asked if there were any casualties, individuals shot, or people bleeding, he kept with the story that he had heard shots and had only stepped out onto his porch after the shooting had subsided. Edward told the 911 operator that it all happened just minutes before and there were bodies left behind from the shooting. The operator attempted to gather more information from Edward, but Edward didn't seem to know where they were shot, the color of their skin, or even their gender. Edward stayed on the phone with her, spinning a convincing tale, until the police arrived.

The first officer arrived almost 30 minutes later, at 2:25 am and the ambulance came shortly thereafter. The sergeant from Precinct 9 had arrived to canvas the scene, spotting Edward standing over Larry. She walked over to Edward, patted him down, and placed him in the back of the squad car for questioning. More police began to arrive on the scene. They witnessed blood-soaked car seats, blood trails running off in different directions, and individuals laying in their own pool of blood. After witnessing that, the chief of police put a call out to his homicide division. Before the paramedics could haul off Andre, the sergeant walked over to him and asked him, "Who shot you?" Andre looked up weakly at her and then at the squad car behind her and said, "You got him."

CHAPTER 7

THE 911 CALL

"I need the police. A man has been shot right outside my door!" The neighbor struggled to say.

"What's your address? Do you need help? Can you see the man?" The operator rattled off questions in between the neighbor's constant and frightful ramblings.

"No I can't see him but I can hear him moaning and calling for help. He's calling for help right outside my front door."

"Sir, what is your name? Can I have your name?" The operator, calm as to not escalate the situation, tried to gain as much information on the situation as she could.

"My name is Oscar ma'am!"

The operator asked Mr. Oscar about the residents of his house and their safety, and whether or not he saw anyone outside near the victim. Mr. Oscar told her that his family was home and safe, and that he did see anyone else outside.

"Where are you now, Sir?" the operator asked with a bit of urgency in her voice.

"I'm inside my son's bedroom. I can see an African American male moving amongst the victims outside. He's wearing a black unbuttoned button-down, over a black shirt with black pants and shoes. He has either braids or dreads pulled back into a ponytail. I can see him outside of my window now, holding a gun downward over the victim, and shouting aggressively. It looks like he might be on the phone with someone".

"You said he's holding a gun?" the operator asked.

"Yes he's standing right next to my gutters with his gun drawn", Mr. Oscar responded.

"Don't go outside of your home Mr. Oscar, officers have been dispatched and should be there soon. Do you have any weapons?"

"No. I do not own any weapons. Please hurry," Mr. Oscar urged the operator.

The police arrived about five minutes later. "Alright, I think I hear them," Oscar said as he walked to his front door. He heard two loud knocks on the door and peered through the peep-hole in the door where he saw two officers standing there in tactical gear. They looked down at Andre for a moment before looking back up at the door. Their weapons were drawn and they seemed pretty tense. "Sir, there is someone bleeding on your doorstep and police were called from this address. Come out so that we may have a word with you."

Only after the cops assured him that it was safe to come out, did Mr. Oscar go outside to meet with the officers. He unlocked the deadbolt, the bottom lock, and removed the stick he had propped up to block entry into the house. Mr. Oscar put on his flip flops and robe and scurried out his front door. He had noticed three squad cars lined up with three more arriving on the scene. The first officer began to question Mr. Oscar about the events that transpired outside his door. He had only witnessed the aftermath of what had happened, stating that he had only seen a young male leaning against his truck wounded before he crawled his way up to his front door. Mr. Oscar told them about how another young male was standing over the young boy with a gun in one hand and a phone in the other and also that the young boy was begging for help and that's why he had called the cops. He noticed that the other young male had signaled over a black car to his location. Mr. Oscar claims that he didn't see the young man get into the car, but he did see the car pass his house and stop at his neighbor's house. However, before the cops arrived, the young man and the black car were gone.

The neighbors were highly disturbed by the blaring police lights and all of the commotion that was going on outside. At 2:30 in the morning, all the residents were standing around in their front yards, trying to piece together a local murder mystery. The street was soon congested with police, fire & rescue, and EMSs. Three ambulances were dispatched to transport the three teens to the appropriate hospitals. The first ambulance tended to Andre because he was in the most critical condition. Mr. Oscar watched as they checked for vitals and loaded Andre into the ambulance. The detectives arrived on the scene and lined little orange cones along a path leading up to Mr. Oscar's front door, outlining the trail of blood and where it originated. Little cones surrounded the area where the car had rolled to and where the other two teens had laid. The sight of the scene was a bit overwhelming for Mr. Oscar as he recalled hearing the sergeant declare this to be the results of a failed armed robbery.

In the ambulance, the paramedics tried to stabilize Andre as he continued to lose more blood. They tried asking him a series of standard medical questions, hoping to get a response but were sadly unsuccessful. Andre was being transported to Gate Way Hospital in Atlanta, one of the leading trauma hospitals in the nation. Upon arrival to the hospital, they rushed him into the ER in the trauma ward, lifting and turning him to assess the damage that had been done. There were several bullet holes on the back of his shirt along with the puncture to his nose and blood running from his mouth. The medical team cut off his shirt, supplied him with oxygen, and began to operate on him, doing everything they could to save his life.

Orandey was admitted to Gate Way shortly after Andre arrived. He was severely injured as well and was taken to the trauma ward. Larry was transported to Well-Care of Atlanta in a more stable condition than the others. He answered all the medical questions while also revealing who had caused the whole incident. Larry supplied them with his name, date of birth, and the names of the other guys that were with him that night. They began to run X-rays and CAT scans on him to assess the damage, finding two bullets lodged in his body, which weren't in lethal spots but they needed to be removed, leading to Larry being sedated. Orandey was also responsive but in a lot more pain and was able to tell the medical staff what they needed to know, and shortly afterward, a call was made to his family.

Just down the hallway from Orandey, Andre was lying on the operating table with tubes protruding in every direction out of his body while a team of fifteen surgeons worked furiously to keep him alive. Andre had lost a lot of blood causing major hemorrhaging but the surgeons were able to locate the bullet in his face and the second bullet in his chest, removing it as quickly as they could to prevent any more blood loss. They had to seal the hole in his chest with a sealant to prevent air from filling his chest cavity. Andre was also shot through the leg where they were able to see both the entry point and the exit point. Looking back at his vitals, the doctors noticed that he was still losing a lot of blood and decided to open up his chest. Andre was bleeding profusely internally and his heart beat slowly fading away.

Down the hallway, Orandey had a similar team of surgeons prepping him for surgery. Countless surgical tools and sanitation equipment was laid out. They examined the bullet hole on the left side of his abdomen, in his neck, and the bullet that struck him in the face. Orandey's blood pressure began to spike as they operated on him, a serious condition to have in the middle of surgery. The surgical team used suction cups to remove the bullets while monitoring his blood pressure. They tried to restore as much facial tissue as they could while also repairing his broken jaw. Orandey was in the trauma ward for two long weeks.

During Orandey's stay, the doctors removed shattered bone pieces, replacing them with prosthetic bone fragments. He was connected to machines that supplied him with oxygen, monitored his blood pressure, and one that checked the functionality of his organs. Orandey went through physical rehab where he was instructed to chew thoroughly in order to build up his facial muscles with the ultimate goal of getting him to swallow. The doctor figured that his life was spared because of the fact that he wasn't shot at close range. And, for the fact that the weapon and ammo used was not of a high caliber. They continued to run tests on him, including a neurological diagnosis to test his memory, reaction time, and deductive reasoning ability. Orandey had chest complications that resulted in a chest cavity that the doctors fixed right up. Although he was in pretty bad shape when he entered the hospital, he was now on his way to a successful recovery. The one thing Orandey could remember most about his experience there was the time he spotted his family peeking into his room. Even though he was restricted to bed rest, he wanted so desperately to just throw the tubes and cables aside and embrace them.

Meanwhile, miles away at Well Care of Atlanta, Larry was being treated for gunshot wounds in the level 1 trauma sector. He suffered from gunshot wounds to the abdomen, left thigh and to the chest. The doctors performed tests and observations on Larry to completely assess the damage he sustained. Several organs (his gallbladder, colon, duodenum, terminal ileum, sigmoid colon, bladder, and femur) were ruptured by the bullet that entered his abdomen, also damaging his rectum. Through a series of operations and surgeries, the doctors were able to save all of his organs, after removing the bullet that was lodged in his body.

The surgical team began to focus their attention to the bullet to his chest, which seemed to have passed right through him because they were able to locate the entry and exit wound. However, the bullet had disrupted his breathing and circulation causing extreme noticeable aggravated breathing. Many more tests were performed after Larry was successfully stabilized, including X-rays to ensure that they had not overlooked anything. It was then that they realized that Larry was hemorrhaging in his left leg where he had been struck by a bullet. Fortunately, it wasn't a hard task for the medical team to stop the hemorrhaging and patch up his leg. After many hours of surgeries and test, Larry was well on his way down the path of recovery

CHAPTER 8

THE CRIME SCENE

"Please return to your homes!" This was the message that repeatedly blared from speakers nestled in the grill of the police cars that lined both sides of the street, all in an attempt to disperse the crowd of on looking neighbors that had begun to gather. Cautions were being taken as to not risk the scene being contaminated or disturbed by influences that were not directly related to the crime. The crime scene needed to remain exactly how the officers found it in order to ensure that the evidence was fresh and untainted. All the crime lab and forensic experts had started to arrive on the scene (CSI, GBI, and forensic scientists, such as forensic entomologist, and forensic psychologist). The detectives flooded the scene questioning any and everyone in sight. They were no longer looking for an armed suspect, they were looking for an armed murderer. The death of Andre shifted the crime from a botched armed robbery to a deadly homicide, bringing in a different team of detectives and officers. The homicide detectives weren't sure who committed the crime, but they were certain that they were going to find out!

CSI collected plenty of blood samples, scraping dried blood into vials to be tested at the lab. Lots of pictures were taken and tons of physical evidence were gathered from the crime scene. Numerous walkthroughs were conducted in an attempt to recreate the altercation while being careful to avoid touching and moving almost nothing. This was done in an effort to construct a crime scene portfolio. Of course, all of this was just step one to a long, tedious process. Only after they were sure that they had photographed everything of importance did they begin carefully prodding and examining objects that could potentially serve as evidence. Cones were lined up in areas of interest and objects were tagged that could serve as evidence and packaged to be examined at the lab.

The next day was all too quickly upon the experts as they continued to piece together the clues. Back at the lab, the forensic scientist went to work, performing blood pattern recognition on the samples, and dusting for fingerprints on the gun, shoes, clothes, and shell casings. CSI carefully studied all of the photos that were taken, piecing together as much as they could.

Detectives were the only law enforcement officers left out in the field at the crime scene investigating potential leads, taping off the whole area, and in some cases, interrogating possible suspects and interviewing possible witnesses, which carried on until the sun had risen. It was a misty Wednesday morning and the detectives were weary after working all night. Around 7:00 am, the tape was removed and the residents were allowed to move about freely. The sunlight emphasized parts of the scene that the dark of night had shrouded. Neighbors were mortified to see blood littered all along the street, especially Mr. Oscar who opened his door only to find that his welcome mat was matted in a pool of dried blood, caking his front porch and trailing down his driveway. Still shaken by the turn of events of earlier that morning and now seeing the blood only worsened his state of being.

The police had dispatched the bioremediation department to clean up the remaining blood who arrived in full biohazard suits, wielding protective equipment specifically designed to prevent contamination. A series of cleaning agents were used to ensure complete sterilization and sanitation. Using the appropriate tools, they ensured the ATP reached 0 before considering their job done. In the end, they removed Mr. Oscar's welcome mat and transported it to their approved biohazard site, where they disposed of a plethora of biohazards. Although all the blood had been cleaned up, nothing could remove the memory of the dreadful events that had taken place in the wee hours of the morning from the mind of Mr. Oscar.

Edward had been taken down to the station for questioning but was released due to a lack of evidence. He returned home, but it didn't take long for the talk to start and for the word to get around. Everyone knew about the party at Keona's, and the majority had seen Orandey and Larry there. No one recalled seeing Andre except for one individual named Boo the friend of Orlando and Orandey. Boo saw Andre when he ditched his bike and jumped into Orlando's car with Orandey and Larry. It was said that they were riding down to Edward's house to get some weed and that was the last he heard from them that night.

CHAPTER 9

LIFE OR DEATH

Gate Way Hospital, known simply as "Gate", is the largest public hospital in the state of Georgia and the fifth largest in the United States. It has the busiest level 1 trauma center in America, supporting downtown Atlanta and the surrounding sub-cities with a total of 953 beds since 1892. Located at 36 Southeast, Atlanta, Georgia, Gate Way was once a segregated institution serving whites in the A and B wings, while serving people of color in the C and D wings. During that time, people referred to those wings as "the Gates" because they were only connected by a hallway known as the "E" wing.

From the time Gates was established up to the present, it has always been a public hospital. Gates accepts patients of low or no income, or insurance, which makes it extremely hard to staff and supply the hospital. Gates rely almost entirely on Memorial West and Pricintion School of Medicine to provide doctor and resident staffing. Financially, Gates rely on Fulton and DeKalb County for funding with occasional donor contributions here and there. Even with the assistance, it is nowhere near fully equipped to serve all of metro Atlanta.

The majority of gunshot victims end up at Gates. Their emergency rooms are always packed, whittling away at their resources. Gates always does good work, doing the best they can with what they have, but unfortunately, not everyone survive. Survival often depends on how fast the victim makes it to Gates after the incident or how quickly they receive aid after arriving. The severity of the wound and the victim's previous health conditions has a great impact on the outcome. Gates has an amazing staff of doctors and surgeons, but sometimes knowledge, skills, talent, resilience, tenacity, or even hope, is not enough to keep one alive.

Andre was transported to Gates because he suffered multiple gunshot wounds. While the team of 15 to 20 doctors labored furiously, fighting to keep him alive, Andre was fighting his own fight to live. Andre's body began to show signs of massive blood loss through skin discoloration and hemorrhaging. The fact that he was still alive at this point was nothing short of a miracle.

Andre's family had arrived at the hospital shortly afterward and was all gathered in the waiting room. His mother and grandmother clutched each other, fearful of what news they might be greeted with when the doctor emerged. All they could do was put their trust in the doctors and comfort each other.

In the operating room, Andre heartbeat had slowed to a stop cutting off all oxygen to the cells and the blood from the rest of the body, expediting his death. His skin began to contract and turn grey, as all of his organs begin to fail. His body temperature dropped rapidly and his skin turned a waxy purple like color. Blood had begun to pool in certain parts of his body, turning the nails purple and places like his hands and feet blue. His body had released his bowels as his eyes rolled to the back of his head. Andre was dead.

The lead doctor, accompanied by two nurses, entered the waiting room to relay the grim news to Andre's family. Their presence quieted the room and froze the grandmother, who had recently been pacing the room, right where she stood. Hopeful eyes were searching, hoping to be met with eyes that told them that everything was okay. Instead, their eyes were met with low, daunting eyes, that cast an ominous mood around their appearance. For a moment, the doctor searched for the right words to say. "We did all we could." He wanted her to know that first because he knew that there was nothing he could say to make the situation better. "We could not save Andre. The cause of death was hemorrhaging." He quickly embraced the mother and grandmother as screams erupted from them, "No, no, no" the two women uttered, over and over again. Other family members wanted to know exactly what happened, shouting it over the cries of the two women. The nurses explained to them what hemorrhaging meant, and how it led to Andre's death. Andre's family was given the privacy of the waiting room, allowing them all the time they needed to grieve.

After spending four hours in the waiting room, the family had calmed down enough to be allowed in the operating room to see Andre. They gathered around the operating table, staring down at the purple and blue body of their loved one, riddled with bullet holes and incisions from the surgeries. In disbelief that this could actually be happening, the sight of Andre in that condition caused them to leave the operating room immediately. Andre's body was admitted to the hospital's mortuary where it was to be kept until funeral arrangements could be made.

CHAPTER 10

THE SURVIVORS

Although Andre's life could not be saved, modern medicine wrote a different story for Orandey and Larry. Immediately down the hallway, Orandey received around the clock medical attention. He was visited daily by his family and friends and was well on his way to a full recovery. Tim Bethel, a local detective, attempted to interview him during his recovery but ultimately had to postpone due to medical reasons. It wasn't until August 5th that the detective was allowed to interview Orandey. The detective met with Orandey at his grandmother's house where he presented him with an assortment of pictures of potential suspects. One particular picture stood out to Orandey more than the rest, and that was the picture of Edward. He picked the picture up and glared intensely at it for a moment as if reliving the moment and sternly passed the photo over to the detective. "It was him!" Orandey said in a cold, dry tone.

Miles away at Well Care of Atlanta, Larry was also experiencing a successful recovery. Doctors were able to remove the bullet in his side as well as the bullet in his chest. The doctors deemed it safer to leave the bullet in his leg, reasoning that it would cause more damage to remove it than to leave it alone. Tons of family members frequented his hospital room up until he was released on August 23rd few months after the shootings. Edward was arrested for the death of Andre and the lethal assault with a firearm against two other individuals, one of those individuals being a minor. He was held without bond and given one free phone call. Edward called home, asking that his mother and brother come to visit him. He later tried convincing his girlfriend to come and see him while he was in holding, but she declined.

Edward remained in holding for many months, declining all plea deals his lawyer offered. He was content with going to trial, figuring he'd have a better chance if he could convince the judge that this was simply a robbery gone wrong. It was a bold assumption, considering the fact that he only had the support of a court-appointed public attorney.

After being released from the hospital, the two young men went their separate ways. Orandey settled down in Florida while Larry went back to live at his mother's place. Larry's mother helped him get back and forth to physical therapy in an attempt to restore his ability to walk again. It took many months before he regained the ability to walk again.

With Edward the local drug dealer incarcerated; Andre the neighborhood's trouble maker buried; and Orandey the party boy absent; the streets were unusually quiet and empty!

CHAPTER 11

TRIAL

"All Rise!"

The crowd filling the Hillsborough County courtroom stood, patiently waiting for the judge to signal for them to take their seats. "Good morning ladies and gentlemen! This is the trial for Edward F. Maxwell on felony charges of second-degree murder, two counts of attempted murder, and two counts of lethal assault by firearm." The Honorable Judge Angela Crawford, presided over the case of The State of Georgia vs. Edward Maxwell. After checking with the prosecutor Ken Benjamin, Judge Crawford prompted the Bailiff to begin swearing in the thirteen jurors.

The Trial

The trial was extensive, covering nine business days between December 7, 2015 and December 16, 2015. Jurors that had hoped this would be a short, one-day trial had their hopes dashed. The jurors were selected at random from a pool of sixty registered voters. Individuals that had some knowledge of the case or events that transpired were automatically dismissed, as well as individuals that were related in some capacity to the victims or the defendant. It was a long vetting process that spanned hours until thirteen unlucky jurors remained. After the selection process, the jurors were briefed by the judge on the official juror protocol. Jurors were expected to be present at 9:00 am with a lunch or a snack because they were expected to be there all day. Jurors were not allowed to disclose any of the information from the case with anyone outside of the courtroom. They were not permitted to do any research on the case or situation and were strictly forbidden from approaching family members, friends, lawyers, or individuals connected to the case inside of the hallways or outside of the courtroom. Any violation of the juror protocol would result in the individual juror being held in contempt of court.

Of the selected jurors, one particular individual felt that he couldn't comply with the strict protocol. "Excuse me. I need to be excused. I'm a doctor and I have to tend to my scheduled patients. These patients need special care, and I'm the only doctor at that hospital with the expertise needed to handle it". The Judge promptly rejected his request to be excused, saying to him, "Sir I'm sorry, but you are going to have to request that they reschedule". Frustrated he replied, "But these patients cannot reschedule, they need specialized care that only I can perform at that hospital". Judge Crawford could see that the doctor didn't quite understand his position. "Again, I apologize, but someone else must see to them. Think about it in this perspective: If you were to suffer from an accident, or take a leave of absence due to an emergency, the hospital would have no choice but to have someone else tend to your patients, correct? Well then simply consider your mandatory civic duty as a juror, as an emergency that you have to handle". The steadfastness of her unwillingness to compromise dashed the hopes of anyone else wishing to be excused. The jurors were released at 5:00 pm, preparing, unknowingly, to embark on a long trial experience spanning the length of nine days.

Day 1 of Trial

On the morning of December 7th, the first day of the trial, jurors shuffled into the courthouse's fourth floor where they were given a parking pass and asked to wait until the trial was ready to begin. The jurors were all seated together and given time to socialize amongst themselves. They seemed to share a common mood amongst them – the feeling of wishing they were not there. Having a long wait time, the jurors shared stories about their professional and personal lives. They shared stories about their children and parents, and about their work and even aspirations. These conversations continued until the bailiff appeared around 1:00 pm, releasing the jurors for lunch. He asked that all thirteen jurors return by 2:00 pm at the latest. The jurors perused downtown Monroe looking for a spot that was close enough to the courthouse, allowing them to return on time. They rallied at a Chick-Fil-a that was in walking distance from the courthouse. Downtown Monroe is a high traffic area especially around that time, so it only made sense that the jurors chose a place within walking distance.

At 2:30 pm, the bailiff returned and led the group to a quaint conference room where they received instructions on deliberating. Each juror was given a notepad and pencil and were not allowed to leave the room during the deliberation. Restrooms were located in the room as well as coffee and water. If anyone had a question, they were instructed to write it down on a slip of paper, knock on the door and hand it to the bailiff. The judge would then write the answer on the slip of paper and send it back. The bailiff informed them that they would be given an hour for lunch and all breaks would be held inside of the deliberation room.

When the bailiff returned, all thirteen jurors were directed to the juror's box in the courtroom. The jurors were allowed to seat themselves in any order they chose and were only allowed to bring a notepad and pencil with them. Stationed to the right and left of the juror's box were the families and representatives of those involved. It wasn't long before Edward Maxwell was escorted into the courtroom. He was well-groomed, sporting a black suit and tie, with his hair pulled back into a ponytail. Edward was accompanied by a representative and a bailiff. After they assumed their spots, Judge Angela Crawford entered the room and the trial officially began. The necessary participants were properly sworn in! "Do you solemnly swear that you will tell the truth, the whole truth, and nothing but the truth, so help you God?", in which they all affirmed, "I do".

The Prosecutor representing the state of Georgia stood and introduced herself before the court, stating that she would be serving as counsel and Attorney for the Plaintiff.

"I am representing the people in this matter, which you were informed during the jury selection a recount of the events that transpired the night of June 13, 2014. Between the hours of 1:30am and 2:30am, three gentlemen, 19 year-old Orandey Mills, 14 year-old Larry Johnson, and 16 year-old Andre Hanks, left a house party and drove to Edward Maxwell's address on 1705 Chapel Hill Road, with the intention of purchasing marijuana from Edward. They had planned on taking Larry home immediately after the party but stopped at Edward's house at the request of Andre who claimed that Edward had shortened him on his supply of drugs."

Andre called Edward Maxwell for weed. Prior to Orandey getting to Ed's house, the plan was to take Larry Johnson home but Andre said his weed was short and he needed a ride to Ed's house. Orandey drove down to Ed's house with Larry on the front passenger side and Andre on the left side in the back seat. Edward Maxwell came out and talked to Andre about the weed being short through the back window then shots rang out.

Mr. Oscar, the neighbor, is a taxi cab driver that lives in the neighborhood. He heard banging on his door and called the police. Tanisha Duncan came home that night from dropping her cousin off at work and saw a black male laying on the curve. She called 911 and continued to drive and saw another body, a young male collapsed outside the vehicle. The third body, which was another male laid out of the car on the driver side.

There are times and circumstances that come about, which in our society would be threatened by acts of violence. This is one of those times. We must safeguard our society; a system of laws has been created to follow. You the jury, are a part of this system of laws. We must hold people accountable. I know you will do your best to judge the merits of this case based on the facts given. This is a case of murder! Later, the judge will give you instructions on how to consider the evidence presented. There is no doubt in my mind, that murder was committed and by the end of this trial, there will be little or no doubt in your mind.

The defendant's attorney Ken Benjamin (opening statement) The laws of a society provides protection for each law abiding citizen. When a crime is committed, it is the state that must apply the law in a manner that offers remedy and bring the guilty parties to justice. But, the law also protects the accused. That is the beauty of the American justice system. We are here to apply the law equally to both sides. The law protects all citizens. In this case, we will show that the evidence the State will produce is deeply flawed. We will show that there is room for reasonable doubt. All I ask of you, the jury, is that you look at Edward Maxwell and remember at this moment he's an American and the system demands you to consider him innocent. He is innocent until proven guilty. He faced the jury with boldness saying, "Edward Maxwell wanted to live from the attempted robbery. He said there was a purchase made by robber one, Andre who came to Edward's house with a gun sitting on his lap, saying he was dissatisfied with the weed he had gotten earlier that day. While robber two, Orandey told Andre "let's go back for a two for one." When they got to Edward's house, Orandey backed into the driveway, shut the lights off and kept the car running. Andre makes the call for Edward to come out. Edward comes out to the car and Andre, robber one, points a 380 in Edward's face and says, "It's a robbery!" After everything had unfolded, it took them one month to arrest Edward.

Edward was acting in self-defense. My client wanted to live. He knew he didn't stand a chance with three guys backed into the driveway with one pointing a 380 in his face, so he reacted to what he saw coming his way. He wanted to live! Thank you.

There were twenty-one testimonial witnesses taking the stand during the trial. All twenty-one witnesses were there to represent the victims of this horrific incident. The defendant didn't have not one witness, nor did he even testify on stand for himself. As the case moved forward, the State called its first witness:

Witness #1 Andres' mom

Ms. Hanks rose up and headed toward the bench. "Please state your name for courts." "Shenell Hanks." "What's your relationship to the victim?" "He's my baby boy, my youngest child." As tears flowed down her face, she could barely utter the words from her mouth. "At the time of this incident how old was your son?" "Sixteen." "Was your son living with you on the day this incident took place? "No, he was living with my mom on Chapel Hill Road."

The prosecutor showed the first Exhibit #1

Picture of Andre Hank, Black African American young male, hair type Afro, skin tone dark, wearing a white T-shirt. It was a close-up head shot of Andre in the photo. Mrs. Hanks burst out in tears – tears she was fighting to hold back since the dreadful walk to the stand. As the tears continued to flow, the prosecutor handed her a tissue. "Prior to the incident happening, when was your last time seeing your son Andre? "May 24th." "When was the final time you saw your son Andre after the incident?" "At the hospital on July 15th when they said he was dead." Ms. Hanks became very emotional. "No more questions," the prosecutor stated.

Defense Attorney Ken Benjamin cross Examines

"Ms. Hanks, do you know what happened on the evening your son got shot?" "No." "Have you ever known your son to have a gun?" "I never seen or known him to have a gun." "I have no more questions for the witness." Ms. Hanks was trembling, walking back to her seat as if her legs were going to give out on her.

Witness #2 Oscar Rodriguez

Mr. Rodriguez was called to stand. However, he needed and interpreter, since the only language he spoke fluently was Spanish. His English was very limited. The Interpreter, Maria M said "please state your name for the courts." He answered, "Oscar Rodriguez" "where do you live?" "1720 Chapel Hill. I live in the house on the corner, last house on the corner lot."

Prosecutor

"Can you please tell us what happened on the morning of June 13, 2014, the day of the incident?" "I'm a taxi driver. I had just come in from work almost 1:15am. I was getting ready for bed when I heard a noise outside my house. I thought it was nothing at first, but it kept going. It got louder. It sounded like chairs or something I left behind my pick-up truck. I went to my son's bedroom window to look out. I then heard a noise screaming for help. I saw a young man leaning over my cab not able to stand, he was bleeding all over the cab. It looked to be a young person. I continued to look out my son's window and I saw another man near the gutter of my home with a gun in his hand. It was a different man with an unbuttoned shirt. It was an adult man looking at the person who was bleeding on my cab. He had a long gun in his hand with a long handle pointing towards the ground. It was about five-minutes of moving back in fourth but I could not understand what was going on. The man that was holding the gun saw a car passing and made a signal with his left hand, but the car kept going. The young man who was bleeding was making his way to my porch, to my front door. He was knocking so I called 911. It took them a while to get there." Maria goes back in fourth in-between words, slowly interpreting to make sure she said every word exactly the way Mr. Rodriguez said it, pausing for breaks, relaying the conversation and continuing until the prosecutor was done with her final question.

"What do you recall telling the 911 operator?" He said, "just what I said here."

Defense Attorney Cross Examines

"Is that what you told the 911 operator?"
The Prosecutor hurriedly objected stating that the DA was badgering the witness. The Judge sustained!

Defense Attorney Continued

"Do you not recall that night telling the operator that the gunman had been in your yard for twenty minutes?" He replied, "No, I'm not sure how long it was but it felt like a long time."
"Did you not tell the operator on the phone that you saw a dark color car pull up in your yard, black or blue in color? You also told them that the man that was holding the gun was not on the phone. You also said you didn't hear gunshots that night. Correct?" Mr. Rodriguez said, "correct I didn't hear no gunshots that night. I told her to send someone out in a hurry, that I was afraid since my house was robbed six months before this incident, they had broken down my door, so I was afraid of what was happening outside." "Do you also recall saying you saw a silver car when asked if you saw any more vehicles?" "I don't remember saying that!" The Defense attorney said "final question." Maria said to Mr. Oscar we are done with questions you can step down.

Witness #3 Tanisha Duncan

Please state your name for the courts! "Tanisha Duncan, I'm the neighbor of Mr. Oscar. I live at 1724 Chapel Hill Road." "What happened the night of the incident on June 13, 2014?" "I called 911 because I saw someone laying in the yard right before the stop sign and then I saw another person laying on the curve on the street."

Exhibit #2 Shows where a body fell from the driver side of the car where a cone was placed, and a second body that fell from the passenger side of the car where there was another cone placed

Exhibit #3-11 Shows the angles of the street and distance from the stop sign to the car, which was all shown to Mrs. Duncan

"Does this look like the scenery the night of the incident?" Mrs. Duncan replied "Yes!"

Defense Attorney Cross Examines

"So, did you see anyone on the street the night of the incident with a silver Toyota Camry?" "I don't recall seeing any other cars on the street. I left my home for about 15-20 min to drop my cousin off at work." "Do you recognize Edward Maxwell as seen here in this courtroom today?" "No, I don't know him," was her reply. That was the DA's final question. Mrs. Duncan exits the stand.

The court was in recess until 9:00AM the next morning:

All witnesses were asked to leave the courtroom first, one behind the other. The jurors were called into the deliberating room and asked to leave their pens and pads in the room and exit. Morning instructions were given for all to return at 9:00 am sharp and to wait in the hallway on the 4th floor for the Bailiff.

Day 2 of the Trial

The morning of December 8th all thirteen jurors arrived on the 4th floor and waited in hallway. It took the Bailiff about an hour to call the jurors into the courtroom. The bailiff came out and did a head count and thirteen jurors walked through the secured doors. In passing, Edward's mom and brother were sitting in the hallway as the jurors passed. Without making any eye contact, they all walked through the secured area into the deliberating room, placing all personal items down and headed out into the courtroom. "All rise!" And then judge Angela Crawford said "you may be seated."

Prosecutor called her next witness.

Witness #4 Sgt. Howard Approached the stand. The bailiff asked her to raise her right hand. "Do you swear to tell the truth, the whole truth, and nothing but truth?" "I do." "Can you please state your name for the court?" "S. Howard." Prosecutor asked her first question, "where are you employed?" "Dekalb County Police Department, East Precinct, 9th Territory." "How long have you been with Dekalb County Police Department?" "Thirteen years. One year as a Sargent Post certified." "How many officers are assigned to you?" "Seven to eight officers per territory." She said that she was called out he morning of June 13th to 1720 Chapel Hill where she saw two bodies before reaching the address, one person on the ground and another standing over that person. She drove to where the man stood then she questioned the man standing, asking him his name. He said, "Edward Maxwell." I then asked "do you know what happen?" He said "No!" I then patted him down and placed him in the back seat of my patrol car, then I went back over to the man lying on the ground. He said, "I was shot." He was conscious and breathing. The EMS unit arrived. When they got there, he lifted his head and I asked him, "do you know who shot you?" He said, "You got him!"

The prosecutor asked, "How are the calls received?" "The 911 dispatcher gets the call, then they're dispatched according to the 911 center that receives it. The information is then entered into a

computerized dispatch system. While on the phone, the dispatcher gets more information to relay to the police, fire department, or EMS who responds and handle multiple calls and prioritize the call that is more of an emergency." The prosecutor then asked about the Computer Aid Dispatch (CAD) report, a printout of the information transmitted to the officer from the dispatcher with respect to any call the police handled. The CAD report was presented to her.

Exhibit #12 showed her arrival time of eleven minutes, it showed that she arrived alone.

Sargent Howard agreed with the report that was placed in front of her. She stated that backup arrived ten minutes after her being on scene. Several other officers arrived shortly after them.

Defense Attorney Cross Examines

He asked his first question about the CAD report in front of her, "Do you show several calls was made?" She then said, "Yes!" "Were either of those calls made from Edward Maxwell?" (The CAD report does show caller name and description of the call). "I do see his name here, Edward Maxwell." "Do you recall writing in your report that the man was standing two feet from the man on the ground?" "I don't recall. I'll have referred to the report I wrote." "What time did you get the call?" "2:15am." "What time did you arrived on the scene?" "2:25am." "No further questions!" SGT. Howard exited the stand.

Witness #5 Officer Fernando Luis

"Please state your name for the court." "Fernando Luis, Badge #32762." The prosecutor asked, "So, where do you work and how long have you been employed there?" "I work for the CDC here in Dekalb County. On October 20, 2013, I was transferred to the East Prescient where I serve the roll as a master police officer patrolling from 10pm-8am." "What do you recall from the night of the incident?" "I was called at 1:30am to 1720 Chapel Hill Road about two males lying in street that had been shot. When I arrived, I witnessed two males lying in the street and there was blood trailing from them to a vehicle that was stalled in the street." The prosecutor rests!

Defense Attorney Cross Examines

"Officer Luis, did you see Edward Maxwell's firearm on the night of the shooting?" He replied, "I can't say for sure if it was Edward's firearm, but I did see a silver and black firearm in the vehicle."

Exhibit #13-16 Pictures of a gun: Photo shows 9mm was on seat it had blood stains as shown in the photos. Photos of the inside of the vehicle were shown with the front door open and the seat and console covered in blood.

Officer Luis stated that he wrote the police report and called the homicide detective to the scene.

Witness #6 Orandey Mills (Victim)

Orandey approached the stand, walking with a limp. He sat as close as possible to the mic because his voice was very distorted. The prosecutor approached the stand and asked, "Can you please state your name for the court?" "Orandey Mills." "Where do you live?" "6263 Presenton Court, the top of the hill of Chapel Hill Drive." "Can you please tell the jury what happened on the night leading up to you getting shot?" "I was getting ready to go to a house party four or five streets down from where I live. The party was supposed to start around 11:30 pm. I was one the ones responsible for setting up for the party. So, I went down to the party." "How did you get to the party?" "A couple of girls picked me up from my house and drove me to the party. We got to the party, so I helped set up. I was in charge to help supply some of the music, so I was loading the music up from the internet to my IPOD playlist to give to Twan. My brother Orlando and friend Boo came up shortly after I got there. Seems as though when they got there, they brought the crowd with them because more people started coming in behind them."

The Prosecutor asked if there were drugs or alcohol at the party. "There were people already smoking weed on the outside with drinks in their hand when I arrived. I passed a few people with drinks in their hands.

More and more people started coming and I started to see people bringing alcohol inside and setting it on a table. My brother Orlando came to me like 1:00am. He seemed a little wasted and was headed toward the door with his keys in his hand. I was like boy where you think you going? You look drunk! So Orlando was like I got to get Larry home. Then I was like man I'll take him, you look to drunk to drive." He then walked me outside to where Larry was waiting by the car.

"My original plan was to meet Ragine at the Waffle House after the party, but his thought was to take Larry home first. I walked around to the driver seat, hopped in, unlocked the door for Larry and he hopped in. He looked fine – he didn't look like he had anything to drink or smoke. Andre rode up on his bike. I didn't see him at all prior to him riding up on the bike. He came over to the driver side window and asked me to take him down street to get some weed to Ed's house."

The Prosecutor then asked, "Did you know where Ed lived?" Orandey answered and said "yes!" "Have you ever purchased weed from Ed in the past?" "Yes, maybe once or twice. I never been up to his door or in his yard. We always met up near the corner of his house." The Prosecutor instructed Orandey to continue. "Andre got in the back seat behind me and we all rode down to Ed's house. As we came up to Ed's' house, Andre asked to use my phone. He said he didn't have one, so I passed him my phone while I backed into the driveway." "Who told you to back into the driveway?" asked the Prosecutor. "No one! I usually back into a driveway – no one told me to that day." Orandey said he backed into the driveway using his rear-view mirrors and never turned around to look at Andre. "I heard Andre on the phone once I was backed in, telling Ed that he was outside. That was all I heard."

"Ed came outside and went to Andre's window, which was the only window down at the time. They were talking from the back window that was rolled all the way down, so they were right there to hear each other." Orandey said that he remembered hearing Andre say something about the weed being short and three seconds later he hears shots. "I tried to pull off and remember being hit, but then I blanked out." He remembered it being the upper part of his body.

"Did you have a gun that night?" asked the Prosecutor. "No, the shooting came from behind me." "Did you see Andre with a gun?" "No, not that night but I have known him to have one in the past."

"What happened next after you believe you got shot from someone behind you?" asked the Prosecutor. "I don't remember. I was out! I started calling Larry's name before I blanked out, but I didn't get an answer. I couldn't see, somehow the car must have stopped. Once the car stopped, I woke up in a daze. I tried getting out of the car but fell right there in doorway, on the ground. I still was calling Larry and he finally answered. I told him to call 911 that I had been shot. He said something like I can't find my phone. I started rolling on the ground. I do remember a little lady standing near me a few feet away from the car saying that help was on the way. I sat still after that. The ambulance came. I was not able to move so they came over to me. All I remember from there is waking up at Gate Way Hospital."

The Prosecutor asked, "Do you remember what you were wearing that night?" "yes, a white t- shirt, white shorts, red hat, and white sneakers." She asked, "Did the Adidas sandals that were left in the car belong to you?" "Orandey replied, "No!" "Do you know what happened to you after being shot? What kind of damage that had been done to your body?" "I was told that I have extensive nerve damage" he replied. The prosecution rests!

Defense Attorney Cross Examines

"Orandey, you said that you live within walking distance from the party?" Orandey answered "Yes!" "So, tell the court why you didn't walk to the party, rather than being picked up by someone." "It was a last minute party that Keosha planned herself because her parents were moving out of the neighborhood and Keisha asked for my help to set the party up."

The Defense Attorney asked, "Did you smoke or drink at the party?" Orandey said, "I smoked a blunt earlier before I got to the party, but not at the party. When I got to the party, I went in to help set up, there was no smoking inside the house, and I had nothing to drink that night." "Did you ever leave the party?" "Yes, I rode with Keosha back and forth to the store a few times to get snacks and pop." "Did y'all purchase liquor that night while out buying things from the store?" "No. The people who were coming to the party were bringing their own bottles of liquor." "Do you recall what time the party ended?" "They were wrapping things up when I was taking Larry home around 1:30-2:00am."

"What kind of weed do you smoke, when you do smoke?" "High grade!" "How much does that cost you?" Orandey replied, "Ten dollars." "So, did you buy one blunt that night?"

The Prosecutor quickly stood saying, "Objection badgering the witness!"

The Judge stated, "Sustain!"

The Defense Attorney moved on to another question. "Orandey, did you know if Andre had a gun that night?"

"Objection!" interjected the Prosecutor.

"Sustain!" said the Judge while banging her gabble on the podium.

"I withdraw! Whose car were you driving the night of the incident in question?" "The car belonged to my mom that was given to Orlando."

The Defense Attorney presented pictures to Orandey in;

Exhibit #5-6 Picture of phone

"Is this the phone you had the night of the shooting?" "Yes!" replied Orandey. "The gun you saw Andre with in past, how did it look?" "From what I recall, it was an all silver gun," replied Orandey. "You told detectives back in August that you never purchased weed from Ed. However, on today, you said to the court that you purchased weed from Ed a few times, maybe once or twice. Is there a reason why you changed your statement?" Orandey then said, "I couldn't remember then." "When you did purchase weed from Ed, where did you get the money from to purchase it?" "I got money from my parents and I saved it."

Prosecutor follow up

"On August 5th when speaking to the detective that came out to your grandmother's home, did you tell the detectives that you believed that Ed was the man who shot you on the night of the shooting?" Orandey said, "Yes!" "Were you shown photos of Ed's mug shot?" "Yes!" "Where are you currently living?" "I moved to Florida." "Do you recall having visitors at the hospital?" "I remember around the end of August or the beginning of September that my Aunt Michelle Simpson came to visit me."

Witness #7 Dr. Skinner Field, MD.

"Can you please state your name for court!" "Dr. Skinner Field."

The Prosecutor asked, "Can you tell the court where you are currently employed?" "Gate Way Metropolitan Trauma Center, in the surgery unit." "Can you please give us your level of certification?" "I graduated from Morehouse School of Medicine in 2002 and have since had ongoing surgical training. I have worked with Gate Way Metropolitan Hospital as an Acute Training Surgeon." "Tell the court what you recall happened on the morning of June 13, 2014?" "May I refer to my report?" Looking over his report, Doctor Field said, "It says here that between 2 & 3am I observed 16 wounds on Orandey's body, throughout his face, left nose, left chest, back, and back area. He was conscious at the time there in the hospital. Physical exams were done on all areas of his body and sent to lab. The Ct Scan and X-rays showed blood hassles. His blood pressure was normal. He was checked for collapsed lungs. Chest X- rays hassling right side 800 high out tube (blood flow). Lungs were functioning. Orandey was bleeding out of his mouth, his heart rate and blood pressure became stable while we treated him. There was a suction tube that was placed in his left neck to clear his airways. No other injuries to left neck, his jaw was broken, and the roof of his mouth was injured. His mid face and right neck suffered minor injuries. He was at Gate Way Hospital for two weeks."

Dr. Field continued, "I also treated Andre Hanks. Based on the report here, it states; His chest tube increased active bleeding 1200 inside tank. He was transported to operating room where he needed more intense care. Report shows that his chest needed to be opened up because he was bleeding uncontrollably. It was reported back to me from the operating room that his heart stopped 1 hour 12 min into surgery. His heart never started again! He was also observed for other injuries – back injuries, his large vessels, and his right atrium, 2 liters of blood loss."

Defense Attorney Cross Examine

The Defense Attorney asked, "Dr. Skinner, how many times have you testified in court?" His reply was "5 to 10 times a year." "What was the cause of Andre Hanks death?" The doctor stated, "He bled to death."

The Defense asked, "Where was he last seen?" "At Gate Way on 5969 Mt. Zion Road." He asked, "So you treated Orandey Mills also?" He said, "Yes, I treated him for three gunshot wounds." "Did you locate the bullets in him?" "No Sir, I didn't."

Prosecutor calls next witness

Witness #8 Dr. Robert G. Graves

"Can you please state your name for the courts?" "Dr. Robert Graves."

The Prosecutor asked, "Where are you currently employed?" He said "Well Care of Atlanta!"

"How long have you been employed?" Dr. Graves replied, "I've been in practice for 25 years as a surgeon." "Did you treat Larry Johnson?" "Yes, for penetrated injuries, gunshot wounds to the chest, abdomen and left leg. A CT scan was done; no arteries were actually bleeding. However, we did determine a vertebrate in the neck was broken causing a spinal cord injury resulting in the loss of sensation. There were injuries, a hole in his stomach, entrance and exit wounds were sealed. He was discharged from the hospital on August 23rd."

Defense Attorney Cross Examine

"Dr. Graves was Well Care of Atlanta previous known as Scott Regional ?" "Yes, they merged in 1997-1998." "What ages do they treat?" "They age out at the age of twenty-one. Larry Johnson being 14 to 15 years old when he was brought in." "What caused him to stay at Well Care of Atlanta longer than usual?" "He was experiencing childlike shocking, combative, causing freighting, and not diffusing well."

Prosecutor follow up

Prosecutor asked, "Was there a psychiatric visit?" Dr. Graves replied, "There were no other changes, so he was released."

Prosecutor Calls next

Witnesses #9 Detective Brandon Baker

Upon reaching the stand, Detective Baker was asked to state his name for the court and his place of employment. "My name is Brandon Baker and I'm currently employed with the Dekalb County Homicide Assault Unit as a detective." "How long have you been with the department?" I've post certified for seven years as a detective." "What was your responsibility as detective on the scene the night of the incident in question?" "I ordered a search warrant on the vehicle and iPhone that was located in the vehicle along with a hand gun and flip flop."

Exhibit #42 Picture of a Vehicle

Defense Attorney Cross Examines

"When you located the phone, was it powered on?" "Yes. It had battery life." "What did you observe on the iPhone that you located?" "A picture of

Orandey Mills was on the front screen." "Were you the one who conducted the search on the iPhone?" "No, it was given to Detective Investigator Norman who took blood samples from the iPhone."

Exhibit #7-15 Photo of inside rear vehicle right passenger, pictures #7 8, 9 & 10

"Do the pictures shown here look like the inside of the vehicle that you took pictures of?" "Yes!"

Exhibit #11 shows where the bullet hit door

Exhibit #13 shows rear seat of vehicle

Exhibit #14 shows hand gun

"Exhibit #14 shows the hand gun that you located on the seat, correct?" "Yes!" The prosecution rest!

The Defense attorney asked, "was ammunition still in the magazine when you located the gun?" "Yes, there were bullets still in the chamber. I took the safety off."

Exhibit #15 pictures of the serial number of a semi-automatic gun

"What can you tell us about a semi-automatic gun?" "The shell gets ejected out. Revolver guns are different the shell doesn't dump out."

Prosecutor Follow Up

"Detective is it possible that the damage on the car door was there prior to the shooting?" "It's possible, but there was a place on the rear door where the gunpowder from the bullet left a stain on the door. I can't say what happened to the other side of the door." "Did you find shells or bullet fragments in the car?" "No!" was the reply.

Witness #10 Officer Angela Morton

After stating her name, she was asked where she was employed and her position. Officer Morton stated that she was a crime scene shift supervisor with Dekalb County. "I have worked as a forensic scientist for seven years and have a BA in forensic science, post certified five years as a supervisor." "What was your job on this case?" "I was responsible for testing all evidence and objects, sending them to the lab for further testing such as blood stain, residue, particles, etc. The blue Honda as shown here in exhibit #14-42.

Exhibit #19 pictures of vehicle

Exhibit #22, 25 picture of Smith Weston

iPhone and green hat was located on front seat.

Exhibit #26 Blue FILA flip flop

"The flip flop was in the vehicle. The Smith Weston had two live rounds in it with blood stains on it. Special Latent finger print powder substance was used to lift the prints. Fourteen prints were lifted. There were no drugs found in the vehicle."

Defense Attorney Cross Examine

"Detective Morgan, are you saying that you found a live round in the gun?" "Yes, it was a PMC brand. There was dried blood on the gun and the safety was not on. The gun was ready to be fired."

Witness #11 India Mason

Prosecutor, "Please state your name for the court." "India Mason!" "Where are you currently employed and in what capacity?" "I'm employed at Well-Care of Atlanta as a Registered Nurse." "Did you work with any of the victims in this case?" "Yes, Larry Johnson as shown here in exhibit #45." I retrieved the bullet from Larry Johnson's body. The bullet was placed in a container at 8:00am on July 13, 2014. The sealed container was turned over to Michael Clark at 8:17am, same day.

Defense attorney cross examine

"How long have you been a nurse?" "Since 1999."

(India Mason was the last witness called for the day) Court was adjourned until 9:00am the next morning. After the witnesses left, a deputy escorted Edward Maxwell back to his cell. The jurors were allowed to leave through secured doors throughout the court room.

Day 3 of the Trial

The jurors patiently waited in the hallway on the fourth floor for the third day of the trial to get underway. At this point, all but one of the jurors were present. Anxiously looking around to see who was missing, they begin to make small talk and wishing this whole ordeal would soon be over. Realizing they could not talk about the trial, they focused their attention on what the traffic was like on the ride to court. At about 9:20am, the missing juror came walking in, apologizing for being late due to the traffic. The others greeted him nervously.

The bailiff returned to the hallway at 9:30am to make another roll call in which all thirteen jurors were accounted for. They were then escorted through the secured doors of the court room. After putting away their personal belongings, they were escorted to the jury box. Edward Maxwell was sitting with his attorney waiting along with everyone for the trial to start for the day.

"All Rise!" The honorable Judge Angela Crawford presiding over the case of Georgia vs Edward Maxwell!

Witness #12 Orlanda James

"Please state your name for the court." "Orlando James." The prosecutor approached, asking the witness to tell the court his relationship to the case. "I'm the victim Orandey Mills' step-brother and have been a part of his family for several years." "Where do you live?" "6263 Presenton Court. We live in the same house together." When asked what happened on the night of June 13, 2014, Orandey responded. He told how he and Larry had been hanging out together most of the day. And that Andre had stopped by wanting a ride to the party. With no room for another passenger, Andre said he was going to Plug's house to get some weed and would meet them later at the party. "Did you see Andre at the party?" "Yes, outside he had rolled up a blunt and we smoked it and he had a Styrofoam cup in his hand." "Do you know how he got to the party?" "No, I just saw him there, standing around." "What happened after that?" "We were just hanging out. We had a couple of drinks later into the party. The later it got, I had a few more drinks." "Do you recall how many drinks you had?" "I lost count after my second drink but I do remember handing over my keys to my brother Orandey to take Larry home."

Exhibit 22 Photos

"These are photos taken of marks shown in the inside door of your mother's car. Do you recall these marks being there prior to you going to the party that night?" Orlando remembered seeing one mark but not the two dings on the door.

Defense Attorney Cross Examines

"Are you presently in school?" "Yes, high-school." "How old are you?" "Eighteen." "So, what time did you get to the party?" "Around midnight!" "What was going on at the party when you arrived?" "People were standing around talking." "Was there smoking and drinking at the party?" "Yes, on the outside." "After you realized that Orandey never returned from taking Larry home, how did you get home?" "I walked!" "After looking at the marks in the photos, can you explain to the court how you believe they got there?" "We were moving my parents and we used a barrel with medal on each end to put some clothes in. We had to force the barrel inside the back seat in order for it to fit." "Did you see anyone with a gun that night?" "No!" "Did you get any weed from Orandey?" "No! I had already smoked earlier?" "So, did you smoke with Larry?" "No! Larry don't smoke or drink. I smoked with someone else."

Prosecutor's Follow-up

"Orlando did you ever discuss this case with any one of the victims?" "No, never."

Witness #13 Larry Johnson (victim)

Larry Johnson, slowly limps his way to the stand. He was asked to state his name for the court. The prosecutor asked Larry his age to which he replied "fifteen!" "Are you currently in school?" "Yes! I attend Mountain View High School." (Larry was wearing his school uniform – green Polo shirt with the Mountain View High School logo patch, khaki pants and black shoes) "Did you attend the party on the night of June 13, 2014?" "Yes! Orlando called my mom asking if I could attend and she gave the ok for me to go." "What happened at the party?" Larry begin to tell his version of what happened the night of the party.

"We were all having a good time walking around talking, listening to music and dancing. I saw a few people from the neighborhood and we chatted. As it got later into the night, I approached Orlando and told him that it was time for me to be heading home. To which he replied man you're right I'll get Orandey to take you since I been drinking. Walking over to Orandey with a smirk on his face, he said make sure you get this dude home. Orlando handed Orandey the keys and we hopped into the car. With Orandey in the driver seat, I got into the front passenger seat. As soon as Orandey cranked up the car, Andre rode up on his bike. He went to the driver side and asked Orandey for a ride up the street to Edward's house to grab some weed. Andre ditched his bike and hopped in the back seat behind Orandey and we all drove down the street to Ed's house. I remember it being the third house from the corner on the right."

The prosecutor asked Larry if he smoked or drink, to which he replied "No!" "Ok continue. What happened when y'all got to Edward's house?" "Andre asked to use Orandey's phone and he asked Orandey to reverse the car in the driveway. Orandey asked why and he said just do it." "Did you know anybody to have a gun that night?" "No! As we sat there a few minutes, a man with twist in his hair came out of the house and walked up to the back window where Andre was sitting behind Orandey. Andre's window was the only one rolled all the way down. I heard Ed ask Andre where was the blunt and he said I don't have it. The next thing I heard were shots coming from the left behind me. I remember holding my stomach because it had started burning. At the time I didn't know I was shot. I begin to raise my knees to shield myself. The car started moving out of the driveway and stopped in the middle of the road. I opened the door, attempted to get out of the car and fell to the ground."

"I heard Orandey calling me but I couldn't see him. After rolling myself into the street, I remembered the same man with the twist grab my hands and started rubbing them all over the gun in his hand. He took out his phone and said 'I just shot these niggas.' Then he walked off."

"Do you know what happened to you?" the prosecutor asked. "I was in the hospital for a month. My spleen and kidney had to be repaired. The doctor said there's still a bullet in my leg but it's best not to remove it. So it's still there."

Defense Attorney Cross Examines

"Larry, how long have you lived in the neighborhood?" "Four years!" "Did you know Andre?" "No. I saw him around the basketball court but I never hung out with him. I did see him around Orandey a few times." "Do you remember giving the detectives a statement after the incident on July 13ᵗʰ?" "Yes!" "Did anyone tell you that if you didn't remember, you didn't have to talk about it?" "No!" "Do you know how many people were at the party?" "There were forty to fifty people, I'm not sure." "Was there smoking and drinking at the party?" "Yes! There was smoking and drinking inside and outside the house." "Did you hear Andre say, "I'm going to get a two for one?" "No, I did not hear him say that. I just heard Andre tell Orandey to back into the driveway. I am sure I heard that." "Are you sure he said that?" "Yes!"

The Prosecutor stood and said "Objection, badgering the witness!"

The defense attorney asked Larry if he saw Andre with a gun. The prosecutor objected to the question. Judge Crawford advised to redirect question. "Did you see Andre pull out a gun and place it on his lap?" "No!"

(The defense attorney and the prosecutor approached the bench and spoke briefly whispering, then returned to their position)

The defense attorney asked Larry if he had visited Orandey since leaving the hospital. "Yes!" "Did y'all discuss the case?" "No!" "Did the white iPhone 4 belong to you?" "Yes!" "Is it the same phone you gave to Andre when y'all got to Edward's house?" "No!" "Do you remember speaking to the doctor in the hospital?" "Yes, I remember telling him that the pain varied from day to day!"

Witness #14 Shantnise Boykin

The prosecutor asked, "Please state your name for the court." "Shantnise Boykin!" Where are you currently employed?" "With Dekalb County as an investigator." She also stated that she has a BA degree from Kennesaw State University here in Georgia. "What do you recall about the night of the incident in question?" "I was dispatched to 1720 Chapel Hill. It was 3:30 or 3:40am. There were no victims on the scene when I arrived. There were three or four houses blocked off with tape."

Exhibit #46 – 79 Photos residence where revolver was located in the grass, bullet fragments

Exhibits #59 & 60 Photos of the passenger side of vehicle

Exhibit #85 Photo of white T-shirt & grey tank top

Defense Attorney Cross Examines

"How many investigative calls do you get a day?" "On average about 250 calls." "What kind of gun did you locate at the scene?" "A 38 Special revolver!" "Did anyone check it for prints?" "Yes! That's common procedure. The 38 hand gun came back with no prints. It was swabbed for DNA. Blood was found on the gun." "Every precaution was taken to avoid contaminating the evidence. And all of the evidence was properly swabbed for DNA then properly stored to preserve all evidence." "What time did you leave the scene?" "7:30am!"

Prosecution Follow-up

"DNA is consisting of body fluids?" "Correct!" "Did you get photos of Edward Maxwell while you were there?" "Yes!"

Exhibits #80 & 83 photos

"Were these photos taken by you (face, body, palms and hands)?" "Yes!"

Witness #15 Detective McCluney

Prosecutor

"Please state your name for the court!" "Detective McCluney!" Detective McCluney proceeded to state his badge number (2455) and occupation as a Dekalb County investigator. "I started as a uniform patrol. In 2004, I became a homicide detective from 2008 – 2014. Currently working as a lead investigator, I deal with twenty-five homicide cases a year. As lead investigator, I follow up with evidence to give reinvent." The prosecutor then asked Detective McCluney to tell the court what happened on June 13, 2014. "I arrived on the scene at 3:30am. Approaching the scene, I saw a vehicle in road with the engine off and the front passenger window was down. I believe the gun was placed in vehicle by whomever was bleeding."

Defense Attorney Cross Examines

"Detective McCluney, did you see blood on gun?" "Yes, small specs on the top." The Defense Attorney asked, "What other part of the investigation did you handle?" "I issued a subpoena to have the phones searched." "And the bullets you found, what happen to them?" "I only found one bullet at the scene."

Prosecutor's follow up "Did you process a warrant for Edward Maxwell?" Detective McCluney explained that the warrant was taken later by another detective.

Witness #16 Carl Duncan

Carl Duncan was called to the stand and asked to state his name and place of employment for the courts. "My name is Carl Duncan and I am currently employed with the Dekalb County Police Department for 22 years. I have been working in homicide for 10 years." The prosecutor asked Officer Duncan to explain the part of the investigation that he handled. Officer Carl Duncan stated that he picked up the Smith and Wesson & Assault Rifle 538 Special and took it to the GBI (Georgia Bureau Investigation) Unit.

Defense Attorney Cross Examine

"Did you handle any other items at the scene?" "No, I never went to the crime scene. I was only in charge of transporting the gun and shell casing." "Do you know if any of these items were tested?" Carl Duncan stated that he did not know and could not say for sure.

Witness #17 Detective Miguel Sanchez

"Please State your name for court." "Miguel Sanchez!" "Where are you currently employed?" "I'm a detective with the Dekalb County Special Victim Unit. I have been a homicide officer since 2014."

"What part of the investigation did you handle?" "I went to WellCare of Atlanta hospital to speak to the victim Larry Johnson, but he was unable to speak at time."

Defense Attorney Cross Examines

"Did you go see the other victims at Gate Way Hospital?" "Yes, I did visit Gate Way Hospital but was unable to interview them." "Police records show that you wrote a report stating that you visited the scene and Rachel, the mother of Edward Maxwell, home." Detective Miguel Sanchez said that he recalled going to Edward Maxwell's home sitting at the table talking to Edward's mother and another person was present, which was said to be her other son, Edward's brother. I do remember searching the gentleman there that had a beard, but I don't recall getting consent to search the home.

Witness #18 Detective Hasan Ahmad

"Please state your name and place of employment for the court." "My name is Hasan Ahmad and I'm currently a detective with the Dekalb County Homicide Unit for four years." "What part of investigation did you handle?" "I took a statement from Edward Maxwell and I also took six pictures of Edward Maxwell."
Exhibit 87 Photo lineup put together by detective Ahmad.

Defense Attorney Cross Examine

"What was your line-up based on?" Detective Ahmad responded, "Skin tone, as well as age and facial hair. In this line-up, I went with lighter to darker shades."

Witness #19 Detective Ramsey

Prosecutor

"Please state your name and place of employment for the court." "I am Detective Ramsey, Badge #2569. I have been employed with Dekalb County Homicide for 11years, a lead detective for 16-17 months. I was the lead detective assigned to this case." "What part of the case did you handle?" "I spoke with two of the victims and wrote the report. I also integrated the process as lead detective with a team of 4-5 detectives assigned to assist me. I went to Gate Way & WellCare Hospital on June 13th. When I went to WellCare to visit Larry Johnson, I spoke with his mom who was there, because Larry was unable to talk.

I also went to Gate Way on June 13th, but Andre and Orandey could not be seen. I went back to WellCare on June 25th and met with Larry Johnson. He was able to talk and his mom and dad were there with him. Larry stated that Edward Maxwell had shot him. I returned to Gate Way on June 25th, Orandey was out of surgery, I spoke with him as well. He says he was shot by Edward Maxwell and referred to him as 'Ed'. I return to Gate Way on June 27th where Orandey was present with his father. While I was there, the conversation was recorded.

Exhibit #88

Taped recording was played for the court.

The Prosecutor asked, "How do you know Edward Maxwell?" "I had been to his house to purchase weed in past. When I returned to the hospital to follow up on the interview, Orandey had been released. He was living with his grandmother at time. I visit him there I collected a DNA swab. He was shown Edward Maxwell in a photo lineup and was able to ID photo #5 as shown here today to be Edward Maxwell. I typed up the report and obtained an arrest warrant. Positive ID's from both victims allowed me to obtain four warrants.

Defense Attorney Cross Examine

"Did you state that you worked at least 100 homicides since being a homicide detective and that you have been with the homicide unit 18months?" "I don't just consider myself an investigator. I'm also considered to be a case expert in homicide." "Did you go to the scene?" "No I assigned my lead detective to go." "Who is the person responsible for assigning the priority cases?" "The case was assigned by a supervisor and wasn't considered a high priority case. This had to be determined by a supervisor. I do not get to choose which cases are high profile.

Orandey raised concerns about the amount of drugs that Andre got versus what he paid for but he never heard them mention a two for1. Larry Johnson told one of my detectives that he heard Andre tell Orandey to back into Edward's driveway. One of my detectives reported that Larry Johnson told him that Andre said there were two bullets in the clip and one in the chamber ready to shoot. Orandey told him that he decided to reverse in driveway himself. Andre just told him pull in and turn the car off. Orandey stated that he did see Andre with a 40 caliber silver gun before this incident. He was asked did Andre point the gun at Edward and Larry said, "No, I didn't see him with a gun."

The Defense Attorney asked, "Whatever happen to the phone records that were ordered?" "The record never came back; it was not able to be tracked down. Larry Johnson told the detective that Ed drove them out his driveway and he also rubbed his hands on the gun."

Exhibit #88 Recording Tape Played

"During your second interview with Orandey, he said he only purchased weed from Ed once. Also, Larry Johnson said Andre told Orandey to reverse into the driveway. But, Orandey said he decided to reverse on his own." "The statements were inconsistent, which most likely led to the reason for not being a high-profile case."

Prosecutor Redirect "Andre mentioned about the 2 for 1. He said Orandey also mentioned during the 2nd recording on June 17th at 4:40am at Gate Way Hospital, that Ed's house got raided before by cops."

"No one could ever confirm that Ed house was ever raided."

Witness #20 Dr. Young

"Please state your name and occupation for the court." "Dr. Young P. Smith. I am a medical examiner and have been since 1995. I investigate the cause of death. In this case, it was sudden death. We did an autopsy, which will gave us the manner of death, history. On July 13, 2014 the exam report history which was performed at the hospital stated that Andre died of gunshot wounds. His body showed the wounds. EMT transferred him to the hospital. I saw where the chest was opened up by the hospital. The left side of the face and left chest was where the gunshot wounds were. The gunshot wound showed that the bullet went through his nose and was found in the left side of his head. The bullet entered through the left chest, went through the lungs, liver and then his heart. There was fatal internal bleeding. The bullet exited the body from the right side. The manner of death was homicide."

Exhibit #99-100 Shows exit wounds

Defense Attorney Cross Examine Exhibit #18-24

"Are the pictures accurate of what you saw on the day you examined Andre body?" "Some of the photos I can identify and some I can't because I testify on several cases a month. I was subpoenaed by the prosecutor's office to be here today. My recollection of the blue hand chief as seen here was on the victim at the time the body reached the autopsy unit. The picture of his right hand had no gloves or bags placed on his hands. As I recall, usually they do in order to preserve the fingerprints. I was not able to determine whether he was left handed or right handed."

Prosecutor Follow up

"Do you know whether the shooter or the body was at an angel?" "I can't give an opinion whether it was or not."

Witness #21 Omar Wells

"Please state your name for the court." "Omar Wells!" The prosecutor asked, "Where are you employed?" "I am employed with the Dekalb County GBI where I work with the Firearms Examination Division."

"Please tell the court how long you've worked in this capacity." "I have worked as an examiner for four years and have analyzed 300 cases. In this case, I analyze two firearms both from the crime scene, along with the bullet casings. I noticed the bullet casing was different on the 40 Caleb and did not match the gun. On the 38 revolver, bullets come out of the cartridge whenever someone empty it."

Exhibit #102 Firearm Revolver was tested

Defense Attorney Cross Examines

"Did the gun have any safety?" "No!"
State Rest No More Witnesses

Defense Attorney Calls his first witness

Witness #1 Victim Larry Johnson

Defense Attorney asked, "Larry, do you know what a Revolver gun is?" "Yes!" "Do you know what an automatic gun is?" "No!" "Did you ride home in the car with Orandey the day before when leaving court?" "Yes, but we didn't discuss the case."

The Defense Attorney calls his second witness

Witness #2 Tyneisha Brown

"Ms. Brown, will you please state your name for court?" "My name is Tyneisha Brown." "Ms. Brown, please tell the court where you are employed." "I'm employed with the Dekalb County Communication for twelve years."

Exhibit #25 Cad Report

"This report shows that the 911 one minute call was made at 2:14am. It was a call to dispatch to 1720 Chapel Hill Dr. Is this the detail report you printed?"

"Yes!"

Prosecutor Cross Examines

Exhibit #25 Full Report
Call Jaminez 2:14am twelve minute call from unknown number; at 2:27 am one minute call; 2:26 am EMS Unit arrive; 2:27 am Police arrive; 2:42 am another EMS unit arrive; 2:44 am another EMS arrives

Defense and State Rest

Closing Arguments

Defense Attorney's Closing Statement

"Ladies and gentlemen of the jury there has to be a General Voir Dire where questions jurors have to address together or individual voice dire when you are questioned as a juror individually. My client just wanted to live! None of the guns belongs to him. There has to be a reasonable doubt that he intended to commit a crime. He was not working off intent. Ladies and gentlemen of the jury, what you need to overcome doubt is fingerprints, DNA, phone records, and gun powder on clothing to prove he intended to kill. We do not have this!"

State Prosecutor's Closing Argument

"Malice Murder can be expressed or implied! Expressed means deliberate intent and implied shows abandoned heart to kill."
Judge gives the law; Law States, State of Georgia v/s Edward Maxwell in Superior Court. He is pleading Not Guilty. He is taking this to trial, so he should be considered innocent until proven guilty beyond reasonable doubt. Reasonable doubt is using common sense. Attack or Believable of the witness of their credibility. Georgia Law does not cause premeditation. Malice Murder beyond Research

Day 4 of Trial

Edward Maxwell was taken back to his cell by the bailiff. As the courtroom was cleared, the prosecutor and defense attorney gathered all the evidence and photos and handed it over to the bailiff. All of the evidence and guns were secured to a wooden board; the sealed envelopes and 107photos were all given to bailiff as the prosecutor and defense attorney exited the courtroom.

The judge addressed the jury, "Ladies and gentlemen you are free to deliberate. You are been given this evidence to help you decide on this case. "Do not omit anything! All twelve of you must come to unanimous decision. "You are allowed to take as much time as you need. If a decision is not made by 5:00pm, the close of day, you will resume on tomorrow at 9:00am. Please feel free to ask me any questions about the law that will help you decide the outcome of this case. The defendant, Edward Maxwell is considered innocent of all charges until discovery without a reasonable doubt. You may proceed to the deliberating room."

Thirteen jurors walked into the deliberating room. It was the third day of the trial and they all looked as exhausted and weary as they felt due to all of the evidence and statements they has seen and heard over the last several days. However, they all knew that the trial must go on.

After one male juror was excused, seven men and five women were charged with the task of going into the deliberating room and delivering a unanimous decision. They were left alone with a dry erase board, marker, note pad and the evidence.

The group decided which one of them would be the chosen one to write on the board. With the board cleared, The chosen one wrote the first stroke on the board only to discover that it was not erasable because they had been given a permanent marker. It could not be erased! Laugher broke out in the room! All might be held in contempt until we got the marker off. That was probably the only laughter during the entire trial. Everything up to this point had been very serious. Within moments all of the jurors took on a serious tone because it was then that they realized that the fate of someone's life was in their hands and that they had to be as human as possible.

Each juror looked over the evidence before passing it on to the next one. With the guns having been nailed to the board, everyone had to be careful not to touch them because the Smith and Wesson still had the bloodstains on the surface of the handle. The bullets were packaged in a gold sealed envelope and labeled. There were one hundred and seven photographs, all of the charges were laid out front, and center with each count listed and what it held.

Each charge was dissected individually, starting with the first listed charge of malice murder. Ten out of the twelve jurors believed that it was not malice murder. There were two who believed that he killed with intent. It was written on board the ten who agreed that Edward Maxwell did not do it with intent; with the other two standing firm that they believed he intended to kill the young men. The jurors deliberated back and forth for hours, looking at the evidence repeatedly. Reasons were shared as to why they believed he did not intend do it. The fact remained that everyone had to go to lunch and return. With no unanimous decision being made on the first charge, it was agreed to table it and move on to the next charge.

While carefully looking over the list of charges, the jurors realized that some of the charges were listed twice. These were considered stacked charges all holding a different count. The grueling task of going through the other nine charges one by one lasted until the end of the day, at which time the jurors revisited the malice murder charge. At 4:40pm, the very exhausted twelve agreed to resume on the next morning at 9:00am.

On the ride home, juror #13 could not stop the events of the day from running through her mind; the up-close photo of Andre's body as he lay on the operating table. The pictures of his lifeless body lying there kept flashing through her mind. The pictures in her head of the bloody scene of the porch and the vehicle were all so vivid in her mind and would not go away. It was as if she was standing there at the actual crime scene. Juror #13 found herself just sitting in a daze at a traffic light that had turned green. To her amazement, people begin honking their horns and yelling, "Move", snapping her back to reality. On a drive home that usually took about thirty minutes seemed to take forever. Taking the longest way home circling a few blocks twice took more like two hours. Going home with the entire case heavy on her mind, all she wanted was for the pictures in her head to go away. She wanted it to be just a nightmare, but she realized that this was very real and that she would have to face the same photos, and evidence all over again the next day. Finally, pulling into the driveway of her home, she slowly made her way from the car to front door. Wearily turning the key in the door, her husband was waiting for her with open arms. He tried everything to relax her, pouring her a glass of her favorite wine, a warm bubble bath, soft music was playing but still, she could not seem to relax. "Baby its going be okay," he reminded her as he massaged her tensed shoulders. He could tell from the look on her face that it had been a rough day. Water begin to fill her eyes as she thought about the very taxing day that she'd had and the long night ahead of her. Her husband tried everything in his power to help her to relax and not let the ordeal of the trial consume her. He tried everything from playing a comical DVD with Lavel Crawford and Kevin Hart to no avail. Eating very little of her dinner that night, Juror #13 went to bed where she tossed and turned, getting very little sleep. She spent a restless night staring up at the ceiling, anxiously waiting for the morning to come. In just a few hour, she would have to get up and go through the same ordeal over again.

Day 5 of Trial

With not much sleep and the events of the day ahead racing through her head, Juror #13 dragged herself to the courthouse, somewhere she had to be having no choice in the matter. She would rather be any place else but there. Arriving there making her way to the fourth floor, going through security it started to fill like a job for her. All 12 jurors met with a cup of coffee in their hands, and bags under their eyes, evidence that they had not gotten any sleep. The bailiff came to the hall and escorted them to the deliberating room. Entering through the secured doors, the room felt cold and isolated with everything being in its original place just as it had been left the day before.

In preparation for the long day that was ahead of them, the jurors brought in different kinds of snacks. By mid-day the snickers, kit Kat, and cokes were gone. The struggle to keep themselves awake was on. The charge of the malice murder was their top priority. Two of the jurors in particular stood out with one being adamant about his decision, the other was a little on the fence. He followed the lead of the others and piggy backed on the words the others spoke. "Edward Maxwell did this with intent." They believe Edward wanted to kill the boys. Believing that Edward did not think twice of a human life, that he did not think the boys would live. They spent hours trying to convince the others why they stood on their beliefs, not looking at much of the evidence, just going off true raw emotions. Although they constantly tried to get them to look into the facts, they had a reason to believe what they felt was true. One went so far to say, "Edward Maxwell deserves the electric chair, he don't deserve to live." He also asked, "Why should he have freedom of life when he has taken someone else's life?"

The other ten jurors could not believe what they were hearing, dropping their heads in disbelief. In that moment, a voice spoke that there was no way a decision could be made. "Let's take a break!" Therefore, all jurors left for lunch. Leaving the room with faces full of anguish, doing everything remotely possible to hold back the tears.

Hopping on the elevator looking straight ahead not making eye contact with anyone, juror #13 knew that if she made eye contact, the tears would flow. Taking a brisk walk through the parking garage, she wanted to get to her car a little quicker. Finally, she was able to shed a few tears. While on her lunch break, she called her husband, dad, brother, nephew, uncle and every black man in her phone list to tell them that she loved them. She called her mom trying to find relief, but her mom could hear the sadness in her voice. She was not able to speak on the situation, so she ended the call quickly telling her mother that she would be fine. Wishing there was a way she could withdraw from it all, she knew that it would not last forever. Taking a bite of her sandwich, she headed back to the courtroom.

Entering the deliberating room, there was complete silence the first thirty minutes. The silence was broken when they started talking about their professions and how they all kind of missed what they did on a day-to-day base. Every one talked about how much work they would have when they did return to work and how they knew they were needed. The college student juror was concerned about getting behind in class and perhaps needing a tutor to get caught up. Talking about their profession, took their minds off the case for a few moments, but they knew it could not last long. They had to get back to deliberating.

One juror opened up saying, "I really thinks Edward was acting in self-defense." He went on to say, "I really think Andre came to rob Edward. The other guys may not have been aware or what Andre plans were, it was matter of being at the wrong place at the wrong time." It only took one juror to state what the others were thinking. Everyone except the two were thinking the same thing. They were not wavering. One stated, "If this was not a matter of intent to kill, why did he leave Andre to die rather than give him aid after he knowingly shot him?" Immediately the other jurors, one after the other begin to give their input. "Edward called the police so he didn't just leave him to die. The report show calls made from Edward's phone number." The opposing juror was eager to say, "He did that only in an attempt to cover his tracks."

Ten of the twelve jurors think that Edward was acting in self-defense while one other could have been thinking it as well, because at times, he agreed to different statements made that Edward did have the heart to just kill the boys he just did not want to die.

One juror that was not in agreement with the others said he needed more time to look over the evidence. For more clarity, the jurors needed to ask the judge a very important question to assist with the decision – Could Edward claim self- defense in his case since the trouble came to his property.

The question was written on a sheet of paper and handed to the bailiff to the judge to answer. "Can Edward use self-defense without premeditated intentions not to kill in this case?" The judge stated that in Edward's case, we cannot use this, although Georgia is a stand your ground state. Edward is a convicted felon who should not be in possession of a firearm because of his prior convictions and the fact that he was currently on probation so that would not be something Edward Maxwell could claim.

Charges

1) Malice Murder, 2) Murder Malice Murder, 3) Aggravated Assault, 4) Murder Malice Murder 5) Possession of firearm by a convicted felon, 6) Aggravated Assault, 7) Aggravated Assault, 8) Firearm, knife possession in commission of a felony, 9) Firearm, knife possession in commission of a felony, 10) Firearm, knife possession in commence of felony

3 of 10 Aggravated Assault charges was the same; to be convicted of one is to be convicted of all three charges. 3 of 10 Firearm, knife possession in commission of a felony was the same; to be convicted of one is to be convicted of all three. There were six convictions! Now down to the last. 3 Murder being 2 of the 1 being Malice Murder.

The jurors had to come to a unanimous agreement. Going into the fifth day, there was still no agreement on the last charge. Malice murder – one juror finally said he would rule out it being malice murder although he felt in the back of his mind that Edward intended to kill the guys. He felt this has been a lengthy trial and he was ready to move on and get this over with because he had grown tired of being there.

The last juror still was not wavering. He said that he believed Edward Maxwell should be executed because he took someone else's life with the intention for him to die, so why should he live. The jurors combed through the evidence piece after piece, reverting to the scene and the second-hand gun. The fact that the gun was there could not simply be omitted as if it was not there. It was a part of the evidence and all of the evidence must be used to decide the case. The gun did not just appear. Whoever had that gun, had intentions as well.

After discussing it for hours, and hearing several personal experiences of being violated or knowing someone who had been, helped get closer to a argument that Edward felt violated, so he acted out of self-defense. Finally, the last juror agreed, stating that if he were left to decide this alone, he would go with the malice murder but to close this case, he would go along with the not guilty verdict because he had doubt on the evidence that this case had provided.

In the end, everyone agreed on all 10 counts.

The bailiff was given all ten counts written on paper to give to the judge. The jurors sat anxiously for about hour waiting for the judge to respond to their verdict. Finally, the judge came into the deliberating room – Judge Angela Crawford stood before the jurors and thanked them for their service. Explaining that the sentencing would be January 28, 2016 in this same courtroom, she invited the jurors to come back to attend.

CHAPTER 12

YOUR RIGHTS

What should readers take away from reading Mid-Night Murder? I would like young people to consider the consequences of their actions when making decisions that can be life altering. Consider what could happen if you attend a party and things go wrong. Orandey and Larry made decisions that were not in their best interest. If young people read this book prior to getting into trouble, perhaps, the incarceration rate in the United States would decrease substantially.

According to statistics, the United States has the largest prison population in the world. 2.3 million Americans are in prisons, 840,000 are black, and 54,148 were juveniles in a juvenile detention center in 2013.

In 2015, The Vera Institute of Justice reported that jails throughout the U.S. had become a warehouse for the poor.

There are a web of entities that profit from the prison system. When Congress passed the Comprehensive Crime Control Act in 1984 as part of the war on drugs.

It is clear that bad decisions were made and it was clear that neither of the young men were monsters. However, their decision brought much destruction to their future. As the reader, who do you believe was the victim in this case? Larry testified on the witness stand that he heard Andre tell Orandey to back into the driveway. However, Orandey contradicted that claim in his testimony when he said that he decided to back in on his own, that no one told him to do so. Did Orandey lie under oath? Do you believe they are all equally guilty? The one who drove, the passenger, or the one who drew the weapon? In your opinion, do you agree that it is just as bad to be a conspirator in a crime as it is to commit the actual crime itself? If you were a juror in this trial, would you have charged Edward with murder?

From the author's perspective, do your research by reading whatever you can about the judicial system. Doing so, will give valuable insight and understanding into the many trials that occur from day to day. Conversations with criminal defense lawyers, judges, and prosecutors can be helpful in understanding these types of trials.

As author of "Mid-Night Murder, I'll be satisfied if the reader develops an understanding about decisions and consequences. If you find yourself entangled in the judicial system, hire an attorney! However, there are good public defenders out there, but it depends on their caseload. Public defenders are an attorney appointed to represent people who cannot afford to hire one.

In the United States, a 1963 U.S.Supreme Court case Gideon v Wainwright ruled that the Sixth Amendment of the Bill of Rights requires government to provide free legal counsel.

Know your rights! And, Enjoy Reading!

ABOUT THE AUTHOR

Roni-Tender Roni is a writer best known for writing stories based on true life events. Born and raised in Miami, Florida, she was one of the fortunate ones to have a very good stable childhood. Although she has seen a lot take place outside her doors as well in the difficult and troubling streets of Miami, she witnessed many of these instances spill over into her older brother's lives. After seeing her brothers and nephews being faced with the criminal justice system she learned how easy it was like for them as young men to grow up without a father's influence.

After moving to Atlanta Georgia and becoming a Dekalb County Citizen she had the privilege to serve as a juror in a high profiled case regarding a juvenile. Listening intently to the details of a murder trial with every piece of evidence in front of her further helped her understand why she never had any sons of her own that would have forced her to her knees to pray. It then became her D.U.T.Y. to reach out and help these fatherless young men. This inspired her to start a nonprofit organization, D.U.T.Y.

Mentoring Program Inc. (Declared Underprivileged Troubled Youth), back in 2017 where she wanted to serve her community and make difference. She was born May 26th 1979 in Miami Florida where her parents divorced when she was two years old. Her life at that age revolved mainly around her passion to read and spend most of her time in church doing community outreach projects. Looking outside her neighborhood taught her who to follow and connect with as well who to pray for constantly. She found comfort in reading which pushed her to discover things about the world beyond what she could have ever imagined especially during the darkest hour of her childhood.

When she couldn't understand why things were so different for kids in her neighborhood than it was for kids that live on other side of tracks she inquired. With so much dysfunction going on outside her doors with drugs, gangs, home evasions, robberies, and abuse etc, it always was an afterthought where one of her mother's children would get trapped in trails of life in city. By the grace of God she was blessed to escape the dangers of life never looking to detour.

She was determined to be the one to make it out and setting that good example since there were not many role models to look up to. Making it all way through high school and into college, avoiding not to become a high school dropout statistic she push her way through and persevered being a teenage mom. She recalled one of her biggest accomplishment walking across the stage nine-months pregnant determined to walk with her class. After going off to college it was a struggle throughout her young adult life knowing she had someone that depended on her with little knowledge of how to raise a child. However, she relied on things she seen her mother do and applied it her child who is a model citizen in her community to this very day. She believes raising girls had to be easier than raising boys from her experience in watching through the lens of the other single parents. Jonnitta Haimes considers herself to be blessed to be able to have experienced the atrocities inflicted on the young men in today's society.

The turning point for her was seeing so many single parents, one being her sister, raising boys watching their court case flash before her eyes contemplating the injustice that may await the outcome of their trial. She knew she need intercede on their behalf and do something before someone close her becomes another statistic

She then involved herself as a community activist and leader forming a organization to serve and render aid to our new generation, D.U.T.Y. Mentoring Program, which is a program to provide mentoring as well as a resolution to the troubled at risk youth. Helping young people one life at time.

Printed in the United States
by Baker & Taylor Publisher Services